Greetings from the shallow end!

I hope you enjoy reading the second book about Electra Brown, *Out of my Depth*.

As Electra's birthday approaches, our heroine is all for an easy life without any aggro. But life becomes crazier not calmer after she launches one of her famous plans, clashes with her dad's girlfriend, and discovers a shocking secret her best friend has been keeping from her. No wonder Electra sometimes feels out of her depth! So, as a way of coping in difficult situations, Electra's mind pops up with gloriously shallow thoughts and questions.

I'm often asked whether these books *are* based on real people and real life. Although the characters are fictitious, they are based on people I've met, and all the mad, bad and sad happenings are taken from real-life situations. Whilst at school I used to sit and stare out of the window dreaming of *anything* but lessons, then go home and write pages and pages in my diary of who did what to whom, and (usually) why wasn't I part of it? Years later, that dreaming and those diaries are brought to life through Electra and her friends.

With love,

Helen

X

More from the shallows of Electra Brown's life:

Life at the Shallow End

Swimming Against the Tide

www.helenbaileybooks.com

OUT OF MY DEPTH

Helen Bailey

*Hodder
Children's
Books*

A division of Hachette Children's Books

Typeset in Berkeley by Avon DataSet Ltd,
Bidford on Avon, Warwickshire

Printed and bound in China by Imago

The paper and board used in this paperback by Hodder Children's Books
are natural recyclable products made from wood grown in
sustainable forests. The manufacturing processes conform to the
environmental regulations of the country of origin.

Hodder Children's Books
A division of Hachette Children's Books
338 Euston Road, London NW1 3BH
An Hachette Livre UK company

This book is dedicated to everyone at Ponteland High School,
Northumberland, 1977–1982, but especially the following:

Helen Aisbitt, Kathryn Aisbitt, Anita Ainsworth,
Alex Gilmour, Sarah Pain, Janice Parker, Gill Pearce
and Lesley Porteous.

Thanks for many happy memories!

Chapter One

Dad puts down his knife and fork and leans across the table towards me. He's always been a bit on the chunky side, but since he left home six months ago his man-boobs have gone up at *least* a cup size, maybe to a 44C, and I'm freaked he'll swipe his pizza topping with them, leaving tomato blotches and a couple of black olives stuck to his white polo shirt.

'Electra, is your mum having actual *relations* with this Phil bloke?'

What?

He may have used the word *relations* but we all know what *relations* mean, especially when said in a low voice with raised eyebrows, and it's so *not* the sort of question most girls get asked by their dad in Pizza Hut on a hot Wednesday evening in June. My parents *never* talk about *relations*, unlike my bezzie Lucy Malone's mum, Bella.

Bella is a *Cool Mum*. The sort of mum who wouldn't bat an eyelid at a mixed sleepover. The sort of mum who discusses the merits of tampons versus pads as if she's discussing whether to buy pink nail varnish or red. Bella may *think* she's cool, but Luce finds talking about sex with her mum excruciating. And I find it shocking with my dad, which is why I gag on a piece of pepperoni from my Stuffed Crust Pepperoni Feast.

Despite the fact that I'm coughing and banging the table and obviously about to choke to death, Dad doesn't yell, 'Is there a doctor in here? My daughter needs help!' whilst he grabs me around the waist and starts doing the Heimlich manoeuvre. Instead, he just stares down at his plate looking sorry for himself.

In an attempt to save my life, I grab my glass of Pepsi and take huge gulps to help the pepperoni down. Unfortunately, at the same time as I gulp *down* the fizzy drink, I burp *up* the mangled meat into a tissue, so the resulting gurp sounds as if some watery alien is living in my chest and about to explode from my mouth in a torrent of froth and undigested food.

'Well?' Dad prompts, totally ignoring the fact that I've pretty much mini-vomited in front of him. 'What's going on with the grease monkey?'

'Don't be so rude,' I snap. 'He's not a grease monkey.

He's an AA man. He rescues motorists in distress.' I'm surprised to feel so defensive about Phil, as I still think of him as The Impostor.

'Huh! He's just a garage mechanic minus the garage,' Dad snorts dismissively. 'You've never actually told me where he fits into things at home. Do you think he's your mum's boyfriend?'

I stall for time by pretending to carefully examine the spat-out-bit of mangled pepperoni whilst I think about Dad's question.

I've never caught Mum and Phil so much as holding hands despite my romance-radar being on permanent high alert. I've tried creeping down the stairs to surprise them; hidden behind a parked car over the road when they've been out in case they were walking home hand in hand and even asked Angela Panteli, who sometimes works as a waitress at her father's restaurant, The Galloping Greek, to text me *immediately* if she spots them canoodling in a dark corner over a plate of stuffed vine leaves and a bottle of something red and rough.

But there's been nothing.

No furtive fumblings or secretive hand-holdings.

No footsie under the kitchen table or sneaky bottom-patting.

They do kiss when Phil comes and goes, but it's

definitely a friendly sort of kiss. The type of kiss I'd give my Uncle Richard or Granddad Stafford. A cheek brush, not a snog with tongue athletics.

But if you're more than a friend but not a boyfriend, what are you? A sub-boyfriend or a plus-friend?

'I think they're just good friends,' I say, rewrapping the mangled pepperoni which is now making me feel really vomity as I've realized just how many unidentifiable bits of pig could be lurking in the pink greasy blob. For all I know I could be eating slices of pig's penis.

'Well, that's interesting.' Dad pushes his pizza away. 'There's something I need to tell you. It's over. Finished.'

I look at Dad's plate. He's barely touched his Deep Pan Super Supreme with extra spicy beef and a side order of garlic bread. Perhaps even *he's* got worried about his expanding moobs and is on a diet.

'Well?' Dad says.

'You could ask them to put it in a box and I'll take it home for Jack,' I say, nibbling at a bit of crust oozing with cheese.

'What?'

'Your pizza. Get them to put it in a box. The Little Runt eats anything.'

'Electra, what *are* you talking about?' Dad sounds irritated and sits back in his chair.

I put on my most withering *Parents can be so thick sometimes* voice and say, 'Duh! Recycling the pizza you don't want.'

I round off this sarky statement with a sneery look, something my other best friend Sorrel Callender excels at, but which she and Lucy say makes me look as if I'm about to sneeze.

For a moment Dad looks confused. Then he says, 'I didn't mean I'd finished with the pizza. I was talking about me and Candy. We've split up.'

One of the most useful expressions to use when dealing with parents is the *totally* blank look. It *completely* confuses the poor dears whilst giving you time to work out your next move.

This is the perfect time for a blank face.

'Well, what do you think?' Dad asks.

It's particularly effective when combined with an *And like do I care?* shrug of the shoulders as then it *really* winds them up.

I do the shrug and blank combo.

'Oh, for goodness' sake, Electra!' Dad snaps. 'I thought you'd be pleased. You hated Candy. Isn't there *anything* you want to say?'

A randomly stupid question pops into my butterfly brain which is *How far can you get a piece of melted cheese to stretch without it breaking?*

I start my cheesy experiment.

Quite a long way actually, is the answer.

'Electra, I'm talking to you,' Dad growls.

'Who dumped who?' I ask, still pulling on the cheese. It's about two garlic-bread bits wider than the pizza plate at the moment.

'Things hadn't been right between us for a while,' Dad replies. 'So I thought it for the best.'

The cheese string I've been testing finally breaks, disappointingly not quite making the third garlic-bread-slice marker. Dad stares down at nothing in particular, the lights in the restaurant bouncing off his almost bald head, highlighting rampant scalp dandruff. The flakes of skin look like white glitter, great in a snow dome, but tragic on the top of your head. He's obviously been using the anti-slaphead lotion again which doesn't seem to help his hair grow, but just turns his scalp dry and flaky.

'So Candy wasn't the great love of your life after all,' I say sarcastically, unable to hide my anger and abandoning the *Am I bovvered?* face for a *Totally Bummed* one. 'You wrecked our lives for nothing.'

I bang my hand on the table for extra impact, but the effect is rather lost as when I bring it back up a big glob of cold stringy mozzarella is dangling from my palm.

When Dad looks up at me he looks sad and lost, as well as porky and bald.

'Listen, Electra, if I could turn back time, don't you think I would?' he sighs.

He waves at our waiter, a skinny Zitty Bum Fluff boy, and signals for the bill.

'Well, if you tell Mum you've left Candy, maybe you could come home?'

Why did I say that? What a stupid thing to suggest! There's *no way* Mum would let Dad waltz through the door as if the last six months have never happened.

I think back to the time when Dad hinted he wasn't getting on with Candy, aka The Bitch Troll. When I'd told Mum, instead of rushing round to the offices of Dad's firm, Plunge It Plumbing Services, throwing her arms round him and gasping, 'I forgive you for being a lying cheating unfaithful rat, just come home,' she'd snapped, 'Good,' and it was never mentioned again.

'Coming home would be great,' Dad says as the ZBF boy comes back with the bill. 'But I can't see it happening whilst your mother's still so angry with me.'

'Maybe angry means she still cares,' I say as Dad slaps some cash down on the table. 'If she really was over you she wouldn't care less.'

* * *

We sit in silence as Dad drives me home in his blue and white van. He and Mum started Plunge It Plumbing Services just after they were married, and although the firm has grown quite big, Dad's never got a proper car, even though he could probably afford something swish and sporty without ladders on the top and toilet-unblocking stuff in the back. He prefers to drive the van as he says it makes him feel like a proper plumber, and with the phone number and website plastered down the side it's a mobile advertisement. I used to be a bit embarrassed about the van and make Dad run me around in Mum's car, but now I quite like sitting up high, staring over the traffic, plus Dad drives like a van driver so he's always cutting people up, making V-signs and yelling out of the window which makes journeys a bit more interesting.

As we pull up outside 14 Mortimer Road, the van towers over Phil Harris's titchy blue Toyota which is parked outside. Phil also rides a Harley-Davidson which he calls The Hog, but we've only seen it once when he came over with it one weekend. It was all throbbing chrome and studded polished leather, and Jack spent hours sitting on it pretending to be a biker, making roaring sounds even though the ignition was switched off.

Jack thinks Phil's the bee's knees because Phil does all the things with him Dad never had the time for, even when he lived at home.

Table football in the house.

Real football in the garden.

Making bits of hutch for Google, our vicious finger-mauling guinea pig.

Showing Jack the huge tool kit he has to carry around in the back of the AA van, which has flashing yellow lights.

And now the motorbike.

No wonder Jack no longer seems to miss Dad. If you're eight years old a man with a fluorescent yellow jacket, an enormous tool kit and plenty of time to talk to you must seem exciting.

Jack might not miss Dad, but I do. So far I've made out to everyone that I'm totally cool with Mum and Dad splitting up, that it's no big deal, I don't care, and I'm *so* not going to turn into one of those whingy wimpy kids who spend their life blaming *everything* on the fact that they're from a broken home.

But underneath it's not true. I do care, *desperately*, and whatever Dad has done and however often he's lied, I miss him.

But now things might change.

He's dumped Candy and more or less said he wants to come home. If I can stop Phil sniffing around Mum the coast is clear for a big parental reunion.

I give Dad a kiss, clamber out of the van, jump down on to the pavement, and wave as he pulls away.

Somehow I've got to get Dad back home.

The problem is, I haven't the foggiest idea how I'm going to do it.

Chapter Two

'I'm back!'

I slam the front door, throw my bag over the banister, and clatter down the stairs to the basement kitchen.

Mum's resting her Mighty Mammaries on the kitchen table, doing a Sudoku puzzle and guzzling a tube of wine gums, whilst Phil is sprawled across the sofa watching tennis on the telly.

He waves when he sees me.

If he wasn't potential boyfriend material for Mum I'd quite like Phil. He's kind, good with The Little Runt, likes rock music, has a great sense of humour, and however much of a cow I've been to him, he never seems to get stressy. But Dad's not going to come home whilst Phil's here, so the first stage in my Get Dad Home plan has to be to get Phil The Impostor to leave. If he's a friend he won't mind butting out whilst Mum and Dad work things out, and if he's a boyfriend, even a sub-boyfriend, then he *definitely* has to go.

'Hello, love,' Mum says, offering me a sweet, which I refuse as I still feel a bit vomity from the pig's-genital pizza.

And that's it.

No further questions.

When it comes to talking about Dad she's as tightly closed as a clam. Whenever I come back from being out with Dad she never asks, 'Have you had a good time?' or, 'How's your dad?'

Whereas Dad continually pumps me for Mum-related gossip, the Queen of the Clams *never* asks *anything* about him. The moment Mum found out about The Bitch Troll she lobbed chunks of cabbage at Dad's head, changed the locks, threw his socks and pants out on to the street so they dangled from car aerials like dodgy flags, and Dad's never set foot inside the house again. Even after all these months Mum organizes Dad's access to Jack via email, making him drop Jack at the bottom of the steps rather than come to the front door. I sometimes wonder if she'd rather Dad was dead.

'Is that the time?' Mum asks no one in particular. 'I'd better drive over and pick Jack up from Daniel's.' She puts down her pen and tucks the tube of sweets into her vast cleavage. She always uses the meeting of the mammaries as a storage area. Shopping lists, bus tickets, receipts, her mobile phone, they all get tucked down there. I don't take after Mum in the boob department. Mine are so small, when I tried putting a pencil between my boobs it shot straight out and stabbed me in the foot. It doesn't help that I'm a mono-boob, the left one being *substantially* larger than the right, which is well odd and deeply worrying.

'Do you want me to go to the Finkelsteins' and get him, Ellie?' asks Phil. 'I'm happy to.'

'No, it's fine. You stay here.' She gets up from the table.

The two of them exchange little smiles. Defo a notch up from an innocent just-friends type of smile.

Damn! Perhaps I haven't been watching hard enough for smoochy signals, and whilst Jack and I were out Mum and Phil have been getting down to *relations*. Somehow I'm going to have to make sure that they're not left on their own long enough for any items of clothing to be substantially rearranged.

'Won't be long!' Mum shouts as she goes upstairs and slams the front door.

It's just me, Phil and the telly.

I look at him sitting on *our* sofa, watching *our* television, drinking coffee from one of *our* mugs, all cosy and settled and at home, even though he has a perfectly good one of his own to go to.

Dad will be back at Aldbourne Road, in that dingy bare flat on his own.

Because The Bitch Troll lived there I've never actually been into the enemy stronghold, so I don't really know that it's dingy or even bare, but given that Dad is the sort of man who would have more fun putting up a wardrobe than choosing it, I doubt it's something out of *Homes and Gardens*. On the other hand, perhaps as Dad bought the flat from Home Malone, the estate agents owned by Tom Malone, Lucy's dad, he asked Bella to furnish it.

Lucy's mum calls herself a home stylist, which means she paints everything cream, dots a few cushions and ornaments around and charges her clients a shed-load of money for doing it. If Bella *has* been involved, Dad's flat will be like Lucy's house, all beige and cream and absolutely terrifying in case you accidentally smear a bit of shattered Flake on the expensive cream linen sofa, or slop some Ribena on an antique rug. Bella is a complete Neat Freak, and poor Luce lives in fear that she's gone to school without remembering to make sure she's hung up her towel spirit-level straight.

Still, bare or beige, Dad is on his own on the other side of town and I'm here with Phil, and if Dad has any chance of coming back, Phil *has* to go. I need to formulate a cunning Evict The Impostor plan. I need to make Phil so uncomfortable he won't want to be around the Brown family any more.

'If you want something else on I'm not really watching Wimbledon,' Phil says, moving up the sofa. 'It's just the highlights.'

I plonk myself down beside him and pretend to stare at the screen. Actually, I stop pretending after about a millisecond, as those grunting guys in white shorts are worth watching with their toned legs and muscle-packed arms.

'Were you out with your dad?' Phil asks.

'Yeah,' I reply, thinking it's a crime that the shorts the tennis hunks are wearing are so baggy.

'That's good,' Phil says. 'Where did you go?'

'Just for a pizza. I nearly choked to death.'

'Someone slip you an aubergine in disguise?' he says, and we both laugh.

He knows that despite being landed with a Greek-sounding name I think aubergines are vegetables of the devil and moussaka should be classed as an illegal substance. Still, the whole Greek-name thing has given me an idea.

I wait until the tennis hunks are changing ends and

rubbing themselves with towels, and then lob the question, 'Do you know *why* Mum and Dad called me Electra?' into the room.

'Because they liked the name?' returns Phil. 'Because it means *The Bright One*?'

'No, because they did *It* in a posh hotel called The Electra when they were on honeymoon in Greece, and then I came along nine months later.' I tell him this with a great deal of relish, even though I don't actually like to think about Mum and Dad having *relations*, as Dad put it.

Phil doesn't say anything.

Fifteen love in the Electra Brown v Phil The Impostor match, although I've sort of got the opening points by deception.

The bit about me being conceived on honeymoon in Greece is true, but the parentals didn't stay in a swanky hotel, but in the Electra Self-Catering Apartments in Faliraki. And the *only* reason they had the ridiculous idea of calling me after the place where they did *It* was because three months before I was born Mum's older sister Vicky had called her daughter Madison, because she and Uncle Hamp were living in a swish place on Madison Avenue in New York. So whilst my Wundercousin swans around New York safe in the knowledge everyone knows she was conceived around money, I'm saddled with a name that's more suited to an exotic dark-eyed Greek girl or a video-vixen, when with my satellite-dish-width pale face, mismatched boobs and mottled salami limbs, I'm *so* not either.

I sacrifice a few moments of ogling at the tennis hunks to swivel my eyes left whilst still keeping my head towards the telly.

Disappointingly there hasn't been any crumpling of Phil's face into a jealous frenzy, and he doesn't seem to be the slightest bit bothered about my tales of honeymoon sex in Greece. Now Stage One of my Evict The Impostor plan has started, it needs to go on, but I'm not sure what to say next. Phil doesn't seem to be easily shocked.

My eyes are swivelled so far left I've got an odd achy feeling above my eyebrows. I don't think I can keep up the *right-angle-to-the-telly-left-swivelled-eyeball* look much longer without serious eye damage. I need to raise my game.

'So, like my name's a constant reminder that they've had *sex*!'

Phil roars with laughter. Annoyingly this probably levels the score.

'Well, doesn't it bother you?' Due to excruciating eye pain I've given up with the sideways stare and am now giving Phil a full-on glare.

17

'Sweetheart, even if you weren't called Electra, I've a pretty good idea that I'm not your mother's first boyfriend.'

My stomach lurches as I realize that for the *first* time, the B word has been used in connection with Phil and my mum.

This wasn't in my plan at all!

I'd been *sure* that Phil wasn't anywhere close to being a boyfriend. How could this have happened when I've been watching them so carefully?

'*Boyfriend?*' I sneer, jumping up off the sofa. I don't want to sit anywhere near The Impostor. 'What makes you think you're my mum's *boyfriend*?'

'Is that such a bad thing?' Phil grabs the dibber and turns the television off. 'I thought you and I got on OK. Don't we?'

'Yeah, when I thought you were like just the odd-job man doing gardening stuff and things!' I realize how cruel I must sound but I can't stop myself. 'Now you've gone from the flower beds to Mum's bed it's a completely different scene!'

'We're still just taking things easy, Electra.' Phil sounds calm. Is there *nothing* I can say that will get this man angry? 'Your mum's still hurting from the divorce. I remember what it was like when my parents split up and when Debs divorced me.'

'They're not divorced!' I snap. 'Remember that! Don't you realize Mum's still married to Dad? You're going out with someone else's wife!'

'Electra, calm down.' Phil pats the sofa beside him. 'Come and sit down.'

'As if!' I practically spit at him.

'OK,' Phil sighs. 'Look, I know it's hard for you to accept, but your mum and dad are no longer a couple. Even if I wasn't here, your dad wouldn't be. He's made a new life with someone else and that's what your mum is starting to do.'

I give what I hope is the ultimate sarky smile instead of the *about to sneeze look* and say in a sing-songy voice, 'Well, that's where you're wrong. Dad has ditched Candy because he's coming back to live here. He wants to make everything right.'

Phil's face is as blank as the TV screen. He just sits scratching his designer-stubble-type beard. I've never bothered about the beard before, but now just looking at it irritates me. Can't he grow a proper one, or does he really think that the half-shaven look suits him? And what's with the short hair? Is he just trying to cover up the fact that he's really almost a coot-head, or does he think that coupled with the skull and crossbones tattoo on his forearm it makes him look tough, just because he's been in the army and probably killed people?

I up the bitch level. If he's as hard as he thinks he is, he can take it.

'You've only known Mum for a few months. Mum's loved Dad since she was sixteen. Sixteen! If she didn't have feelings for him she wouldn't be angry with him, she wouldn't give a flea's fart about him! She *still* loves him!'

Phil just sits there, scratching his stubble.

I go in for the kill.

'So if Dad wants to come back, and Jack and I want Dad back, why are you even bothering to keep sniffing around here?'

Finally Phil's face crumples, and he seems to slump so far into the sofa it looks as if he's about to be engulfed by the blue woolly throw and a set of red scatter cushions.

Game, Set and Match to Electra Brown! I think to myself. Re-sult! The Impostor has *finally* got the message he's not welcome around here!

'Tell your mum I'll ring her.' Phil's voice is a hoarse whisper as he heaves himself off the sofa.

I watch him trudge up the stairs and hear him quietly close the front door behind him.

As his car pulls away I should feel triumphant. Pleased that already my plan to get Dad home is underway. Proud of myself that I've made it crystal clear to The Impostor that he's not welcome in our family.

But I don't feel proud of myself.

I feel tearful and a prime bitch.

Chapter Three

As I hurtle out of the end of Mortimer Road, the bus is already waiting at the bus stop in Talbot Road.

I try shouting and waving my arms as I run towards it, but I'm not surprised to hear the hiss of the doors closing. Even if you bang on those doors with tears in your eyes, *still* those evil bus drivers won't open up. You can hear them cackling like hyenas as they pull away, leaving you stranded on the tarmac, late for school, and facing the beady eye of Mrs Jones, the school secretary who keeps the late register and doesn't think *Slept In* is a valid excuse for being late.

I *hate* getting up for school at the best of times, but I didn't sleep well last night and feel *totally* wasted. I kept having nightmares about Phil force-feeding me pig willy and aubergine pizzas as punishment for being such a total bitch to him.

22

When Mum came back with Jack and asked where Phil was, I fibbed and said he'd had a call from his office about some big emergency where loads of cars had broken down on the motorway because of the heat, and he'd been asked to go and sort it out. I waffled on a bit about engines overheating and tyres melting on the hot tarmac and she seemed to fall for it. As I'm my father's daughter I've obviously inherited his easy ability to lie and, like him, I'll worry about being found out later. If the worst comes to the worst I'll swear blind that's what Phil told me, so it'll be his word against mine. It'll be interesting to see who Mum believes.

Anyway, the combination of being naturally lazy and not sleeping because of the porky nightmares meant that I was knackered by the time the alarm went off at 7.30. I hit the snooze button so many times that even doing without hair-washing, a double spray of deodorant instead of a shower and no breakfast I was cutting it fine to get to the school bus on time. And now it's pulling away and I've missed it.

But then the bus stops.

As I gallop towards it, the doors open, and I practically fall up the step and straight into Claudia Barnes who's leaning against the plastic window separating the bus driver from the passengers. Her chest is thrust so far forward I'm convinced that if she jiggled around a bit she could polish the screen with her boobs. No wonder me, Sorrel and Luce have nicknamed her Tits Out. Whatever she does, however she's sitting, standing and for all I know lying, she always thrusts her boobs so far out her shoulder blades practically touch at the back.

This thrusting of the mammaries divides the pupils of Burke's down the middle, it being a source of fascination for anyone who's male, and a source of irritation for the rest of us who are convinced that Claudia's really flat-chested, but has padded out her bra with fake baps, the silicone ones that look like skinless and boneless chicken fillets and sit by the till at La Senza.

It's *so* annoying that boys are so shallow as to be interested in something that would almost certainly come apart in their hand if they got to the grappling stage. For heaven's sake, some of them even think she's a born blonde with naturally straight hair! Can't they see her hair is attacked by straighteners on a daily basis, and regularly drenched in peroxide? The fact that her hair doesn't match her dark eyebrows should be a clue. Actually, they probably don't notice the eyebrows. She's plucked them so much there's just a single line of hairs and lots of dotty black bits where the hairs are coming through. I always think of them as a line of ants marching above her eyes.

But, and this is a *terrible* thing to admit even to myself, even though I can't stand the way Tits Out is just so *obvious* when it comes to boys, sticking her chest out, laughing at their really weedy jokes and tossing her bleached hair, deep down I'm sort of jealous of the way boys flit around her like bees to honey.

I did once say this to Sorrel, but she was very sniffy about the whole thing and said it wasn't so much bees around a honeypot as flies around cheap meat, so I've never mentioned it again.

I've tried the whole shoulders-back-tits-out thing, but Luce says I seem incapable of jutting my shoulders back without my mouth going into some sort of weird spasm and my eyes going bug-eyed. I'm not sure that the bug-eyed-spasm look is going to do anything to increase my success rate with boys, which on a scale of one to ten, one being that you have done absolutely nothing, nada, zilch, not even holding hands, and ten being you've gone all the way (or at least have enough experience to *pretend* you have) currently stands at about minus three or, should I say, *sans trois*.

This is because my experience with boys was totally blighted just over a year ago by a French exchange student called Didier Deville. DD must be the only French boy in the world who can't French kiss, unless

French kissing is vastly overrated and really does consist of being smothered in spit whilst having to listen to a noise like water gurgling down a plughole.

Perhaps if I'd been able to speak the language I could have asked him whether he was sure he was doing it properly. I may have given myself a minus score on the experience scale, but I'm pretty sure that having your make-up washed off by Froggy saliva isn't right, but unfortunately as my French is crappola and he couldn't understand my English above the spit and suction noise, I didn't get a chance to ask him. Annoyingly, Mademoiselle Armstrong, our big butch Geordie French teacher, has never given us the French translation of *Please stop licking my face*, which is just *so* typical of the teachers at Flora Burke's Community School. They never teach you *anything* useful.

Of course, throughout the entire French exchange, Tits Out had badges of slaggery on show where the froggy vampires had locked on to her neck and left a necklace of hickeys. I didn't want a row of hickeys, but I would have liked the *opportunity* to have had one.

'Thanks for waiting, Steve.' Tits Out bats her spidery triple-mascara-coated eyelashes and gives a pouty smile to the sweaty-looking bus driver who, worryingly, seems to be looking at Tits Out's tits rather than the road, even though the bus is now moving.

'Thanks, Claudia,' I gasp, the last-minute sprint having knackered me.

'I saw you coming so I asked the driver to wait,' Claudia explains as we ignore the stony glares of the wrinklies on their way to work on the lower deck.

I follow her up the stairs to the top deck. She's hitched up the hideous green tartan kilt we have to wear, so instead of looking like a giant green checked blanket wrapped round her waist, it's more like a little flippy micro-skirt. I'm shocked to see that under the micro-kilt she's wearing a tiny red thong, giving me an eyeful of parts that only doctors should see so early on a Thursday morning.

The top deck is filled with the white shirts and green ties of Burke's pupils.

At the back is Sorrel who lives five stops further along the route from me, and in front of her is Claudia's bezzie, Natalie Price.

Natalie is peering into a tiny handbag mirror, piling more thick make-up on her spotty face. The amount she uses she probably single-handedly keeps Maybelline in business. *I* think she thinks it hides her zits, but really it just makes her face look yellow and greasy. Secretly, me

Sorrel and Luce call her Butterface, but over the last few weeks she's been experimenting with fake tan. This has turned her skin a weird muddy colour, but combined with the yellow make-up she still insists on trowelling on, her face is now like a huge lumpy pumpkin. I might suggest to the girls that we call her Pumpkin Head, just for the summer.

Claudia slides in next to Butterface and I sit behind, next to Sorrel.

'I saw Electra was going to miss the bus so I asked the driver guy to wait,' Tits Out explains to no one in particular as Butterface hands her the mirror.

Sorrel throws me a sideways *Why?* look and I shrug. There's been plenty of mornings where Tits Out could have asked one of the bus drivers who drive route 210 to wait for me, so why today?

She must have noticed our glances in the mirror as she swivels round to face us.

'God, you two are *so* suspicious!' she says, her hands fluttering around her neck. 'Can't I do a good turn without there being like some deep reason?'

'Sorree,' I say. 'I'm just feeling double-trashed this morning. Dad wants to come home so I'm going to try and get him and Mum back together.'

'Blimey, when did your old man spring that one on

you?' Sorrel asks. 'I thought once they'd done a runner, they'd gone for good. That's what my dad did.'

Five years ago, Sorrel's dad, Desmond, left her mum, Yolanda, older sister Jasmine and younger sister Senna to live in Barbados where he's an artist. Yolanda then met Ray Johnson, a weedy little man with a ponytail who works in a camera shop, and had the twins, Orris and Basil. Sorrel's still angry about it, but then she's angry about *everything*.

'I thought he'd gone too, but he told me he'd dumped The Bitch Troll when we were having a pizza last night,' I say. 'I was going to text you and Luce but then I got in a sort of fight with Phil.'

'Are you going to help the reptile slither home?' Sorrel asks.

I shrug and stare at the front of the bus where some poor little kid is being forced to wear his shirt inside out whilst someone else is trying to pull his trousers off.

If I could turn back time to pre-January 2nd this year and Dad could come home and everything would be like it was before, then I'd have him back like a shot. Then I wouldn't know anything about him leading a whole double life until he finally got caught out.

But I can't turn back time, and if he does come back, can I forgive and forget how he lied to us, over and over again? More importantly, could Mum?

The bus rattles on towards school.

I text Luce to tell her we're on our way, even though I'm going to see her in about twenty minutes and she'll know we're on the bus, whilst Sorrel frets that one of her beaded braids is already coming undone, less than a week after spending five hours sitting in the hairdresser's.

Butterface is piling on more concealer. Without a mirror she's just feeling where the lumps are, using her fingers to pat orange gunk on the swellings.

Tits Out has her back to me and is peering into the mirror, plucking her eyebrows. Every time she grabs a hair she licks the end of the tweezers and eats it.

One of the most annoying things about Tits Out, other than her boobs, her hair, her eyebrows and the fact that she's far more successful with boys than I am, is that whatever you've done or are about to do, she's been there, done that, bought the T-shirt and has almost certainly worn it.

Her mum and dad divorced a few years ago and she's now got a stepmonster, a stepführer, several step-siblings, half-siblings and one proper older sister. When my parents first split up she drove me mad with her continuous *Oh, I know all about broken homes* type comments, but perhaps she might be able to help me with my parental reconciliation plan.

'What do you think, Claudia?' I ask. 'Is it worth concocting a cunning and devious plan to get the parentals back together?'

'Total waste of time.' She swivels round to face me and drops her tweezers into her pencil case. 'I know all about trying to get the old folks back together, and I'm telling you, Electra, once they've wrinkled the sheets in someone else's bed, there ain't no going back to the marital one.'

This is deeply depressing, but I'm not going to let Tits Out put me off my cunning, but as yet unplanned plan.

'Well, as far as I know, Phil and Mum haven't been wrinkling any sheets, so I could at least give it a go.'

'It won't work,' Claudia says firmly. 'They're not bald eagles.'

'What have slap-head hawks got to do with my parents?' I ask, thinking Tits Out has totally lost it, the peroxide probably having soaked into her brain.

'Bald eagles mate for life,' she says in a tone of voice which implies *Surely* everyone *knows that!* 'They're like totally faithful. They don't shag another bird unless their mate dies. Can't say that for humans, can you?'

It's depressing, but she's right.

Tits Out starts fiddling with the collar of her shirt, tugging it up and down. Perhaps she has a badge of slaggery which she's trying to hide. That would make a change. She usually makes sure that *everyone* can see she's been neck-sucked, proudly displaying the bruises whenever she gets a chance.

And then I see it.

I've been so stressy-headed over my own problems I hadn't noticed it. But there it is. Circling round her neck, falling to a low, large bump nestling between the fake baps, where it hangs, quivering.

A school tie.

Not the foul green polyester noose we wear at Burke's, but a navy and red silk tie. A tie belonging to someone from King William's School for Boys, the testosterone-packed talent-soaked private school just near my dad's flat.

No wonder Claudia got the bus driver to wait for me! No wonder she kept fiddling with her neck, drawing attention to it! Claudia Barnes wanted as many people as possible to see that she's in possession of a trophy tie!

'Where did you get that?' I gasp, realizing, too late, that I probably should have played it cool and acted as if I hadn't noticed, or if I had, that I couldn't be bothered and like *totally* don't care.

The ant eyebrows march upwards as TO gives an unconvincing impression of not knowing what I'm talking about.

Sorrel is *still* staring at the beads on the end of her braids. I've a feeling that she'd already spotted the tie but was determined not to give Tits Out the satisfaction of appearing interested.

As I've already blown any pretence of *Am I bovvered?* it's too late to turn back.

'Duh, the tie, Claudia. Who gave you the tie?'

Tits Out looks down at her chest and pretends to be totally surprised that she's found herself wearing a tie belonging to a completely different school, and not only that, a tie from an all-boys' school!

'Oh, this old thing?' she says casually. 'Jags gave it to me.'

My stomach turns over so violently I really think it's going to leap up out of my body and hurtle through my mouth, splattering Tits Out and Butterface with undigested pig's-penis pizza and body gore.

Jags – or Javier Antonio Garcia to give him his full and glorious proper name – defines the phrase *Spanish Lurve God*, except he's not from Spain, he was born in Slough.

His father is a doctor and *is* Spanish, which is why Dr Garcia's DNA has given his son the most gorgeous dark eyes, long eyelashes, jet-black hair, which is always gelled to a little peak at his forehead, and just a hint of proper stubble on his olive skin, rather than the pathetic thin wispy stuff that the Zitty Bum Fluff boys at Burke's grow through their pussy spots.

He's not particularly tall – Sorrel is a bit sarky about that and has recently started calling him El Dwarfo – but then she's sarky about anything to do with boys, so I don't let his lack of height worry me. As far as I'm concerned, he's perfect. The total Lurve God package and the top scorer on my Snogability Scale.

Luce and I spend *hours* talking about the S-Scale, and although Sorrel does sometimes join in, she never gives *anyone* above a 1.6 so I don't think she takes it seriously.

The Snogability Scale has five main divisions:

1S – Not snogging but mouth-to-mouth resuscitation. When I was in the Brownies we did a first-aid course where we had to clamp our smackers around the lips of some life-sized rubber doll in a tracksuit to pretend to bring it to life. That *definitely* didn't count as snogging, not unless you're a bit of a weirdo, although thinking about it, Didier Deville obviously modelled his snogging technique on bringing a plastic doll to life there was so much gasping and smeared saliva.

2S – Snogging for totally unselfish reasons, e.g. to prevent global disasters. In other words, the only way the lips of a 2S boy would get anywhere near me is if someone said, 'Electra Brown! You've got to snog this 2S boy otherwise the world will explode *immediately!*' It would be a pain and I'd have nightmares afterwards, but at least I would be forever famous as the girl who saved mankind from extinction by unselfish snogging.

3S – The most boring score. Neither one thing nor the other. Snogging a 3S boy doesn't bring someone to life or save the planet, nor is it particularly enjoyable. It's OK if you do, OK if you don't. The sort of boy who would have a 3S score is the sort that you might snog just to keep your lips in practice, but only so as you can move on to someone better ASAP.

4S – Only one whole number between a 3S and a 4S boy, but that one number separates the boring from the beautiful, the men from the boys so to speak. 4S is a *serious* snogging score. Lusted after by masses of girls, bagging a 4S boy would instantly catapult you from the middle-to-low-popular category of girl to a popular Princess of Cool. Unless of course you're Tits Out, and then you'll always be a sleazer, whoever you snog.

5S – The Oscar of the snogging world. There is no higher achievement than being awarded a 5S for your snogging. Like movie stars, 5S boys are only obtainable in your dreams, even if you do see them riding their bikes around in real life. Cool, sporty, gorgeous, a couple of years older, probably Spanish and *definitely* at another school, it's unlikely you will remember anything beyond the first brush of a 5S's lips as the sheer shock of contact with such a perfect physical specimen is bound to cause instant collapse at their feet.

The scores we award are constantly under review. For instance, someone who has scored a 3.8 but then gets a tan and scores a goal in a football match might find himself a 4.1, only to lose a few points when it's winter, he's pale, and he's dropped from the team for being rubbish.

With 41 possible scores between 1 and 5 you can see why we spend so much time discussing it.

Anyway, the one person who never wavers from being a perfect 5 is Jags.

I've loved him for ages, learnt Shakespeare quotes to impress him, run through cornfields with him holding hands, frolicked in the sea with him, spent hours at the sports centre for him and even picked out our engagement ring, a huge diamond blingtastic knuckleduster-type thing which would make Claudia Barnes shrivel and die of jealousy.

There's just one problem.

All this happens in my dreams.

In reality he's never said a single word directly to me,

not unless you count, 'Watch it!' said in a less than loving way when I crashed into him in the dark whilst I was wearing a borrowed Arsenal woolly hat and daggy clothes, and he was pushing his bike because my little bro had stolen his bike lights.

He sees Luce quite a lot because Jags and her older brother James both go to King William's, not that this connection has helped me snare The Spanish Lurve God in any way. In fact, I think knowing Luce has actually hindered my chances as instead of being seen as a foxy little minx by Jags and the KW boys, James just refers to me as 'A friend of my kid sister', which is always said in such a demeaning and offhand way, it makes me feel like I'm still in nappies with a dummy rammed into my mouth. No wonder Jags won't talk to me.

He's obviously said plenty to Tits Out, and maybe even *done* plenty to her if she's wearing his tie.

I want to lean forward and strangle her with the tie but, so she thinks I don't care, I use the sullen look I usually keep for the parentals.

'Why'd he give it to you, Claudia?' This comes out as a rather embarrassing high-pitched squeak.

'To celebrate finishing his exams,' Tits Out says as she strokes the shimmering navy silk with her extra-long French- and Tippex-manicured talons.

I wonder what else she might have stroked to get her hands on this trophy tie.

'But it's only the end of June!' I say, forgetting the rule that the more you pay for education, the less time you spend at school.

Claudia looks smug. 'He's taken lots of GCSEs a year early so he's pretty much finished school. He'll text me if he needs it back.'

She tosses her bleached hair, but as it's so stiff with styling gunk, a bit sticks out like straw and points towards Natalie's ear.

Text her! This is getting worse. Not only does she have his tie, she has his moby number! I'm not sure how my fantasy parallel life of having Jags as my boyfriend is going to cope with the *devastating* news that he's been unfaithful with the Queen of Sleaze.

Butterface/Pumpkin Head lets out a big sigh, but her face is so caked with make-up, her expression doesn't change from its usual gormless look. Whatever Natalie is feeling or saying, her face remains blank. I used to think of it as a death mask plastered in Maybelline, but now, with the new fake tan regime, it's more *Still life with Pumpkin*.

'I had a tie too, from James Malone, but his mum found out and he had to get it back,' she sniffs. 'I'd got

Shimmering Strawberry lip gloss on it and Mrs Malone made James pay for it to be dry-cleaned.'

I'm sunk into even deeper gloom. It's deeply depressing that I'm not even a tiny blip on anyone's hot totty radar whilst zitty gormy Butterface is deemed worthy of a trophy tie, even on a temporary basis.

The bus lurches to a halt outside the sprawling mass of flat-roofed grey concrete buildings that makes up Flora Burke's Community School. I can't get down the stairs and off the bus quickly enough.

I'm standing by the school gates gulping in great lungfuls of warm air when Sorrel catches up.

'You should have just ignored the silly cow,' she says, scowling. 'She was *desperate* for someone to notice that freakin' tie and you fell right into her slaggy trap.'

'Thanks for pointing out the now blindingly obvious,' I groan.

Lucy bounces up looking every inch a Princess of Cool, all tall, blonde, gorgeous and toothpaste-white shiny. Even if I hadn't missed my shower I still wouldn't look shiny. Shiny-faced yes, but in an oily rather than glowing way. And Luce's gleaming smile reminds me I didn't brush my teeth this morning so I've probably got rampant parrot breath.

'You OK?' Lucy pats my shoulder.

'No,' I grumble.

I go to unhook the face-lengthening chandelier earrings I usually wear on the way to school, but realize that as I was so late I hadn't put any in, not even the little fake diamond studs I wear for lessons.

Can the last twenty-four hours get any worse? I'm in turmoil over Dad, I'm upset over Jags and now I have naked ears.

'What's wrong this time?' Lucy asks.

'Her cheating old man wants to crawl back, the grease monkey is fiddling with her mum's spark plugs and El Dwarfo has been groping the Queen of Sleaze,' says Sorrel.

Couldn't have put it better myself.

Chapter Four

We've skipped school lunch as it's one of the days when they're only selling healthy stuff like salads and nut rissoles, and bought stuff from Flyin' Brian who used to be at Burke's, but got expelled for supergluing shut a classroom door, unfortunately when the pupils and a teacher were still inside it. He's supposed to be home-schooled with special tutors, but he's obviously never at home as he now makes tons of money selling chips, burgers and the odd can of cider through the railings at lunchtime. So, having stuffed ourselves with grease, we're now lying on the grass underneath the windows of the science block, soaking up the blazing midday sun, our bags scrunched up under our heads as makeshift lumpy pillows.

I love warm weather, but summer isn't my favourite season from a fashion perspective. I'm built for wrapping up in cold weather not stripping off in hot.

I suppose if I was all willowy and gorge like Luce I might not mind having to abandon the thick black tights which cover the sturdy salami legs and hold everything in place, or the jumpers which disguise my mono-boobitus, or the long-sleeved shirts that hide my arms, especially my left one with its dodgy henna tattoo. It was supposed to be a butterfly and temporary, but bits of the butterfly have faded at different rates, so now it has a body but no wings or antenna and looks like a giant mouse turd. But I'm not a modelly skinny-minnie type, so I do mind having to strip off.

On the other hand, with her sort of bod, Luce could easily peel off without fear of ridicule or humiliation, but she's lying on the grass next to me, all prim and proper as usual, her shirt tucked in and her sleeves only rolled up to her elbows.

Sorrel and I have our ties off, our white shirts unbuttoned as far as we dare, the sleeves rolled right up and our skirts round our thighs, though my hands are hovering near the hem in case a boy comes past and I need to pull it down. I don't want even the ZBF boys to see my sturdy upper thighs, plus I'm already going pink in the sun even though we've only been out for about twenty minutes. It's all right for Sorrel to fry herself. Being of Caribbean extraction she's got built-in factor 50. She can lie and fry with her tummy out, her chromium belly bar glinting against her dark skin, without risking first-degree sunburn.

'God, if Poxy Moxy is down as my teacher for Year 10 I'm defo going to drop history,' I say squinting up into the sunshine.

It's been a tough morning sitting in sweltering classrooms, first with some supply teacher droning on about sciencey stuff, and then a double period of history with Mr Moxon, aka Poxy Moxy, a man who looks like he died and was buried years ago but has risen from the dead to teach us. His eyes are sunken, his cheeks are hollow, he has a few strands of dyed black hair scraped across his dome-like head, and when he bares his teeth (in a smirk, never a smile) they look like little yellow pegs.

I'm not surprised he's a history teacher. He's so old he probably fought in the First World War.

History lessons are pretty dire, but I told myself that I could put up with them because Poxy Moxy was bound to drop down dead at any minute, and there's nothing like a dead teacher slumped on the floor of the classroom to add a bit of spice to a lesson. But now, almost a year later, I've decided Mr Moxon is one of the living dead, so I've stopped waiting for his voice to go into a death rattle, and even though I put *heat* magazine in my folder and prop it up so Poxy can't see I'm reading about fashion disasters rather than world conflicts, I'm still bored.

'What would you do instead of history?' Lucy asks.

I stare up at the blue sky dotted with clouds which look like cotton wool balls.

'Quadruple geography,' I sigh. 'Just so as I can stare at Buff Butler all day.'

After The Spanish Lurve God, Jon Butler, our geography teacher, is the next most gorgeous creature to walk the earth, not counting completely unobtainables like footballers or film stars.

I don't usually go for blonds, but I make an exception for Mr Butler. He's definitely at *least* a 4 on the S-Scale.

He's tall, young, gorgeous and has an amazingly neat muscly butt. Towards the end of a lesson, when he's scribbled all over the board and is having to bend down to write on the bottom, he really sticks his bum out towards the class, which is quite something to see, especially as it looks as if he goes commando under his chinos. I'm sure he swings free because even when I've sat at the front of the class to get a really good look, there's no visible underpant line. He could of course be wearing a thong, but even on a man as gorgeous as Buff that's a disgusting thought.

Amazingly, whilst I didn't consciously try and learn geography, some of it must have passively filtered into my brain, because since Mr Butler became our teacher my grades have shot up. Gorgeous Buff gave me a quite good report. He told Mum that I was *eager*, which is true, though obviously not for the reasons he thinks. Mr Butler probably assumes I'm sitting at the front of the class gazing at him because I'm fascinated by his teaching, not realizing I'm trying to work out his underwear situation and his Snogability Scale score.

I've chosen geography as one of my GCSEs, but I'm freaking out at the thought that he might not be my teacher next term, as last week Butterface, who has a *mega* crush on him, told him that she would only take geography in Year 10 if he promised to be her teacher. To everyone's total horror, Buff said that the timetable was being fixed over the summer so he wasn't sure whether it would be him that would be teaching the first year of GCSE geography or Miss Rogers who's known as The Hamster because she's got such fat cheeks.

I was there when Natalie asked him, and her usually totally expressionless face fell and she *definitely* went pale beneath the orange fake tan and yellow make-up.

Being taught by The Hamster would be a *total* disaster, as not only would the lessons be dull without the teacher eye candy to perk things up, my grades would plummet. At least when Mum goes on about how disappointing my report is, at the moment I can say, 'Except in geography,' and I need all the help I can get when it comes to school reports.

I'm not a natural student, and for years I made a big fuss about going to school.

I absolutely hated it and registered my protest by being a master bunker, somehow getting 'lost' between closing the front door of my house and walking through the school gates, strangely finding myself wandering around the shops at Eastwood Circle Retail Park, telling the security guards in New Look that the teachers were on strike or that there'd been an asbestos scare and we'd all been sent home.

Just when I was running out of excuses and was seriously wondering whether they might be convinced by 'An alien spaceship has landed on the playing field and the whole school is cordoned off!' if I said it in a suitably hysterical way, I read an article in a mag which completely changed the way I felt about school.

The article said if there was something you really really hate, something you're forced to do and can't get out of, then change the way you look at it.

Reframing they called it.

So whereas before I thought of school as seven hours of torture, now I look at it as seven hours of spending time with my friends with the odd lesson thrown in, like a sort of all-day social club.

The getting up in the morning is still a drag, the uniform is tragic, some teachers are complete monsters and however much I try and reframe games, standing outside in a tiny skirt which shows off my mottled salami limbs whilst our lesbionic games teacher yells instructions is still dire, but otherwise it's a breeze. Homework can always be done at the last minute, and if you don't know the answers there's usually some geek on the bus you can force into giving you theirs. I don't have to worry about really serious exams (mocks don't count) for another two years. I might not do much work now, but I'll pull out the stops just before the real exams and it will all be OK, or at least that's what I keep telling Mum when she goes on at me.

We've just gone through another phase of her going *on* and *on* about school and how I'll end up with a crappy job whilst everyone else is going off to university, which is *completely* the wrong thing to say, because as soon as I can legally leave school I'm off. I'm not sure where I'm off to, but I'll worry about that later. Sorrel wants to go into the police, and Luce is so gorgeous she doesn't have to worry as she's bound to marry a rich footballer and live in a house with a heart-shaped swimming pool.

Also, as I'd like to point out but don't dare, neither Mum or Dad went to uni, and up until the point when Dad ran off with The Bitch Troll and Mum was so heartbroken she drank too much red wine, popped happy pills from Dr Chaudhri and screamed all the time, they hadn't done too badly for themselves.

Maybe if Buff *isn't* my teacher next term I can get the parentals to ask him whether he would give me some *private* tuition.

I'd need to think carefully about my wardrobe as usually he only sees me in daggy uniform, so extra tuition would be the ideal opportunity to show him just how stylish I can be, and how my face looks a little slimmer with dangly shoulder-skimming earrings and the right make-up.

My daydream about having one-on-one private lessons with Mr Butler is rudely interrupted by the bell for the next period.

An hour of physics and then the ultimate in academic torture, French.

We haul ourselves to our feet and rearrange our clothes.

I've got big green stains on my elbows so I'm going to spend the afternoon fantasizing about how Jags managed to get through the school gates just to roll on the grass with me.

Whilst there are some real downers to starting Year 10 next term, like the beginning of proper GCSE coursework and the fact that there is no guarantee Poxy will peg it or Buff will be my teacher, there are several good things, such as we'll have some free time which the school calls 'Study Periods' but which are just really a chance to sit quietly in the library and read *Teen Vogue* wedged in a copy of *National Geographic*.

The other great thing about leaving Year 9 behind is that Mrs Frost will no longer be my form teacher. She might still teach me as she's also Head of English, but at least I won't have to see her twice a day, at the start when however much you reframe school there's still a whole day to get through, and like now, at the end of the day, when you'd rather be tearing out of the school gates and bolting towards freedom, the shops and television.

I can't stand her.

It's a boiling hot day but Frosty's still dressed in her usual penguin get-up of black skirt, black cardigan and white shirt. The saddo is even wearing tights with her sandals, and the heat must be making her water-retention problem even worse because her ankles are *gi-normous*, spilling over the top of her fatty-splatty trotters, which I'm sure are webbed. The ankle and foot combo was quite big this morning, but now, after a day standing around in hot classrooms, they look like elephant's feet.

Frosty the Penguin has just taken the final reg and we're like coiled springs, ready to hurtle out of our seats, when she squawks out, 'Claudia Barnes. Whose tie is that you're wearing?'

I groan inwardly.

I've been trying to ignore the tie issue all day and have completely banished it from my Jags daydreams, as even my shallow but overactive imagination hasn't managed to come up with a suitably innocent explanation as to how the Queen of Sleaze got her hands on a bit of Jags's wardrobe.

Claudia goes all pouty.

'Oh, Mrs Frost, I lost mine last night.'

The class giggle at the thought of what Claudia might have lost the night before, not helped by the fact that Tits Out wiggles her baps and flutters her mascara-drenched eyelashes.

I don't giggle.

I fume.

Claudia touches the tie in a way which looks as if she's pointing at her chest and says, 'A very good friend of mine lent me his.'

I could have forgiven the fish guzzler's sense of style if she'd snapped, 'Claudia, you are obviously a tie tart with dyed hair and a dubious chest, take it off now!' but all Frosty says is, 'Get hold of a proper one as soon as possible, Claudia. See you tomorrow, class.'

'Lucy! *Je suis ici, ma chérie!*'

As we stream out of the school gates a woman with a neat blonde bob and big diamond studs in her ears leans out of the window of a large silver Range Rover and waves what I know will be a perfectly manicured hand in our direction.

It's Bella Malone. The Neat Freak. Lucy's mum.

Luce smiles and waves back at her mum and says through perfect but gritted teeth, 'I *so* wish she wouldn't do that.'

'More private tuition with Madame La Poodle?' asks Sorrel.

Lucy nods and sighs. 'Mum just doesn't understand I'm not good at French. Or maths, or English or...'

'*Allons! Allons!*' Bella's shrill voice cuts through the school-gate chatter.

Sorrel is in the top French group, Lucy is struggling to stay in the middle set and I'm in the bottom dreggy one, but even I can tell that '*Allons! Allons!*' means Bella is trying to hurry Lucy up, though the pipping of the horn at the same time is a bit of a giveaway.

Bella's been arranging extra French lessons for Luce as her school report said that she might have to be moved to my dreggy set which means she won't be able to take French GCSE a year early and can never get above a grade C. According to Luce, her mum is trying to 'immerse her in the French culture and language', which means garlic in everything and even the odd snail on toast. Apparently Bella keeps trying to speak French to Lucy at home which means poor Luce spends the entire time just going, '*Oui*' or '*Non*' because that's all she feels confident about saying.

The family go to France every year for two weeks at the end of August, but this year Lucy's dreading it as it's not really a holiday, just a chance for Bella to force more French phrases down her kids' necks.

'At least when Michael was around there was only a one in three chance I'd be sent into a shop to ask for something I didn't want in a language I don't understand,' Lucy had moaned when she'd told us that her older brother Michael has decided to stay in London after his first year at uni finishes, as he'd rather work in Starbucks than come home. 'Now with just James, it's one in two!'

There's more impatient beeping from the silver 4x4.

Luce gives us both a hug and heads off to French torture. As the car pulls away I'm sure I can hear French accordion music coming from inside.

After school, Sorrel and I ended up getting a bus to Eastwood Circle and just wandering around, gossiping about whether short men can still be Lurve Gods (we differed on this one: I said defo, but *only* if they looked Spanish, and Sorrel said no way, *especially* if they looked Spanish) and whether Sorrel should ditch the braids and have her hair relaxed and straightened.

I didn't buy anything because I haven't much money at the moment, having spent it on things like shoes I can't walk in, jeans that were already a tad too tight before they went in the wash, and belts that emphasize the fact that I've got no waist, just an area between where my boobs should be and my bum. Anyway, with my birthday only being a couple of weeks away I'm hoping for shed-loads of cash.

Mum and Dad promised me my own laptop for my birthday, but that was before Dad walked out, so I'm not sure whether it's still going to happen. I hope so. I'm completely fed up of having to try and wrestle Jack off the computer. It's not as if The Little Runt does any proper work on it. He only ever plays games, which means I can't get on to surf and look at well-odd vid clips on YouTube and MySpace, not unless I beat him up to get him off.

Sorrel bought a family-sized bucket of KFC and, although I had a few bits of chicken, she devoured most of it with astonishing speed.

Sorrel *loves* meat in the way that I love Jags.

In other words, she thinks about meat, dreams about meat, and spends a good proportion of her life working out ways of actually getting some meat.

This is because her mum is a total lentil and has banned the family from eating flesh. Some years ago she declared their house a *Face Food Free Zone*, which I think was the final straw for Sorrel's dad, who left after he was caught secretly eating a bacon sarnie in their back garden.

The lack of meat doesn't seem to worry Ray, probably because instead of craving meat he lusts after cars like Bella Malone's Range Rover, even though Yolanda calls 4x4s Beast Cars and people carriers, Beast Buses, and spends a good deal of her time slapping *Gas Guzzler!* stickers on them. The family doesn't have a car, even a little one, because Yolanda believes they're killing the planet, so she'd chuck Ray out if she knew he'd been secretly test-driving mega Beast Cars at the local garage.

It's not just the humans in the Callender-Johnson household who have to forgo flesh. Even Parsley the cat is forced to eat soya beans mashed up with veggies instead of normal fishy cat food. This causes it to fart continuously and go into the garden to murder anything that moves.

Every time Parsley brings some half-dead barely-flapping-on-its-last-cheep bird into the house and Yolanda gets upset, Sorrel goes mental and points out to her mum that if humans (and cats) weren't biologically meant to eat meat then they wouldn't have gastric juices capable of dissolving tough bits of flesh, or even pointy teeth to rip it apart. Yolanda just ignores her and keeps cooking soya burgers and bowls of brown rice that look like maggots, so Sorrel spends all her money on meaty meals in KFC or Burger King, and bottles of meat-breath-masking mouthwash in Superdrug.

Yolanda makes sure *everything* is recycled. I don't *ever* go to the loo in either Sorrel's house or The Bay Tree Café, the organic café Yolanda runs. Not because of the after-effects of so much fart-food, but because the loo paper is so recycled it's *really* rough, and you don't end up wiping so much as exfoliating your bits. Not a good feeling.

Anyway, we wandered around until the shutters started coming down on the shops, then we got on the bus.

Sorrel got off before me and *then* I realized I should have phoned Mum to say I was going to be late.

Chapter Five

'Sorree,' I say, dumping my school bag on the kitchen table and opening the fridge. 'I meant to phone.'

As I take a glug of Sunny D straight from the bottle, pouring some of it down my white shirt, I notice Mum glaring at me. If looks could kill, by now I'd be slumped on the terracotta tiles with my head resting against the salad drawer in the fridge.

'I just forgot the time!' I say. 'Don't stress! I've eaten some KFC so it's not like I need tea.'

I shove the bottle back in the fridge, and go and flop on the sofa.

The atmosphere is tense. Mum's obviously annoyed I didn't phone her to say I was going to be late, and it irritates her that I drink straight from the bottle, even though I think she should be grateful it saves on the washing up.

'Why did you lie about why Phil left last night?'

Oh. My. God.

With stressing out about Tits Out and Jags I've *completely* forgotten that I was supposed to come up with some plausible explanation as to why I was a premium bitch to The Impostor, and why I lied to Mum about the reason he left.

I dip my head down so my fringe covers my eyes and peer at Mum from under it. There's a bright-red flush heading at great speed from the nipple end of her Mighty Mammaries, up her cleavage and towards her neck. Whatever excuse I come up with had better be good if she isn't to spontaneously combust.

I keep my face totally blank and play for time by asking as innocently as I can, 'Why? What did Phil say?'

'Phil . . .' Mum is practically hyperventilating, 'Phil said that you were very rude to him and he felt he had no option but to leave.'

The sneaky tattooed rat!

I'm furious!

I'd counted on Phil not squealing on me if he was hoping to keep on seeing Mum. Now I know he's a snitch, he's got *no* chance!

'Actually, Electra, he didn't say that. I guessed. But I can tell from your face I'm right, aren't I?'

Damn! A double bluff by Mum and I've fallen for it. Even though my eyes are obscured by my fringe, my face obviously wasn't as blank as I'd intended.

I sink further down in the sofa and grab a cushion. I don't know what I think a cushion in front of me will do, but somehow it seems to help buffer me from Mad Mum who's starting to rant.

'I rang Phil to find out about how he'd got on last night after he'd left. He said he didn't know anything about being called to a mass breakdown on the motorway. He laughed when I mentioned the melting tyres. Apparently they don't even melt in the desert, let alone on the outskirts of an English town.'

I squeeze my safety cushion. Now I'm not just annoyed with Phil, I'm mad at myself for being so amateur in my lying. I knew adding that extra bit about the tyres melting was a mistake. Why didn't I just keep my big gob shut and stop at engines overheating?

'What did you say to him, Electra?' Mum is standing by the sofa, her arms folded across her big baps. She seems a tad calmer.

I shrug.

'I said, WHAT DID YOU SAY TO HIM?'

Then again, perhaps not.

Hearing shouting, The Little Runt comes belting down

the stairs into the kitchen just as Mum is yelling, 'I will not have any more lies in this house, do you hear me?' which is *such* a daft thing to say, as of course I can hear her. She's standing next to me, bellowing in my ear.

'Has Poo Head been lying?' Jack's eyes are shining at the thought of his big sister being in trouble. There's almost five years between us and as he's a total pain, if it wasn't for the fact that he lives under the same roof as me, I'd have *nothing* to do with him.

'Shut up, you little scroat!' I snap back.

'Liar! Liar! Big pooey pants on fire!'

Jack leans over me on the sofa so we're practically eyeball-to-eyeball. He starts making one of the stupid faces he's always pulling, so I grab his head like a football and drag him over the top of the sofa, kicking and screaming and crying. Mum comes over and pulls us apart, and The Little Runt clings on to her, still sobbing.

'She attacked me!'

Sob sob sob. It's pathetic.

'You deserved it, you snivelling scroat!' I scream at him, noticing a long bit of yellowy-green snot is dribbling from his nose.

Jack stops crying and starts pointing at my chest and sniggering. At first I think he's laughing at my mono-boobite situation, but then I look down to see not only is there an orange river of Sunny D running down my white shirt, there's also a sort of yellowy-green stain right by my left boob.

The Little Runt has snotted on my school shirt!

When he sees me notice the snot stain he sticks his tongue out and laughs, so I chuck the safety cushion at him but miss, and hit Mum in the stomach.

'Stop it! Both of you!' Mum looks like she means business. 'Jack, go upstairs and play in your room.'

'But I want to play football!' The Little Runt whinges.

I just can't look at him in case there's more dangling bogeys.

'Then go into the garden!' Mum barks.

'But you said go to your room and my room's not in the garden,' Jack grumbles as he stomps up the stairs and out of the back door.

I go to get off the sofa so I can change out of the multi-stained shirt, but Mum stops me.

'Sit down.'

'But . . .'

'Stay right where you are, young lady. Now, what went on between you and Phil yesterday?'

I give my best *sullen/shruggy/blank* look.

'Well then. We'll sit here all night.'

She perches on the arm of the sofa and takes a boiled

sweet out of her cleavage. The secret sweet store means Mum really *could* be here for ever, and I just haven't got the stamina to face a parental stand-off still wearing a contaminated garment and after a day of devastating Jags and Tits Out news. Anyway, I want to get out of my school uniform, change into something summery and cute but which doesn't show my meaty upper arms, make my sturdy legs look bigger or my bum huge, and go and accidentally on purpose walk past the sports centre in case The Spanish Lurve God is there playing tennis. I haven't time to spend all evening staring at a wall whilst Mum stares at me whilst Tits Out is getting more bits of Jags's wardrobe to parade on the bus tomorrow morning.

I give a big sigh so Mum realizes I'm only doing this because I'm being interrogated and practically tortured for the info.

'He said he was your boyfriend and I just pointed out that you and Dad weren't divorced yet and perhaps he should back off a bit. Or words to that effect.'

As her face still looks close to exploding, I decide to miss out the bit where I mentioned her bed and flower beds.

'How *dare* you say those things to Phil!' Mum shrieks, abandoning the sofa arm. She starts pacing around the kitchen. 'Don't you think it's up to *me* to decide whether Phil should "back off a bit" as you put it?'

'Oh, great! So what I think doesn't count?' I drag the throw off the back of the sofa and wrap it around me it like a woolly cocoon.

'I didn't say that, did I?'

Mad Mum is still pacing, doing circuits of the kitchen table behind me. What with being a bit of a porker, she used to move about very slowly, but when Dad left and she lost all the weight she speeded up. Since meeting Phil, she's been munching the carbs recently so she's put a bit of weight on again, but she's still pretty speedy.

'When have I *ever* not taken your feelings into account, Electra?'

I shrug, but as I'm wrapped up so tightly in the blue blanket I don't think the shrug was noticeable. Also, wrapping yourself up in wool is not a particularly bright thing to do on a hot summer's night, and I'm now beginning to sweat like a pig, despite the double spray of deodorant this morning.

'I thought you liked Phil. I thought you didn't mind him coming round here and helping out.' She unwraps the sweet and rams it in her mouth, crunching it. If she's not savouring confectionery she must *really* be angry.

'That was before . . .'

I stop myself.

I wasn't going to tell Mum the Dad and Candy break-up news until it was the right moment, and I'm not sure that being wrapped up like an Egyptian mummy whilst Mum jumps about the kitchen like a box of mad frogs is the setting I'd been hoping for.

She veers off from one of her circuits and comes over to the sofa, looming over me so that her Mighty Mammaries are pointing towards me like a couple of torpedo missiles, primed and ready to fire. She may have lost weight over the last few months, but those puppies are still *huge*.

'Before what, Electra?'

How am I going to get out of this one?

'BEFORE WHAT?'

Might as well go for it. No time like the present and all that jazz.

I pull the throw even tighter around me for protection and say, 'Before Dad kicked out Candy because he wants to come home.'

If Mum's boobs *had* been a couple of torpedoes, I have no doubt that at this very minute she would have fired them so that whatever is in torpedoes would be ricocheting around the kitchen, bouncing off the magnolia walls, and peppering my body with mammary shrapnel.

'He said *WHAT*?'

She doesn't wait for me to answer.

'How dare that unfaithful lying reptile use you to ferry messages around about his seedy love life!'

Hmm. This isn't going well. I should have stuck to my original plan of waiting for the perfect moment to spill the break-up beans.

'It *so* wasn't like that, Mum!'

'Do you really think that after all that's gone on I'd have that slug back? I'd rather stick hot pins in my eyes!'

'Er . . .'

'What sort of a man talks to his teenage daughter about coming home before he talks to his wife? His thankfully soon to be ex-wife?'

'Well, if you'd let him in the house, maybe he'd tell you himself!' I yell.

Mum stomps over to the other side of the kitchen and pulls the cork out of a bottle of red wine. It's already been opened, but if it wasn't, she's so mad I could imagine her ripping the cork out with her teeth and spitting it on to the floor.

'So is this what this has been all about?' The red wine is now in a glass, but only briefly, as Mum is glugging it down as if it's weak Ribena. She's already on a refill by the time she says, 'You think that if Phil wasn't here then your father could come home?'

'Well, to state the obvious, Mum, Dad's not going to come home if Phil is practically living here, is he?' I snap.

'Listen, Electra, whether Phil is here or not, I never *ever* want your father back, do you understand?' Mum is really shouting now, and the wine in the glass is slopping over the edge, splashing her white V-necked T-shirt. It looks like she's been stabbed in the stomach. 'I don't want that man anywhere near this house!'

'But it's not just about you, is it?' I scream back.

I go to jump up from the sofa, *completely* forgetting I'm bandaged in blue wool, so end up sort of hopping around like a kid in a sack race as I try to untangle myself.

'*I* want him back! *I* want him to be able to come to the house. Now that you're so lurved up with Phil you've forgotten about what *I* want. You don't care about me. You only ever think about yourself! You're just totally selfish!'

I run out of the room, up the stairs and out of the front door, slamming it as hard as possible behind me. It's not a good thing to do in an old house which already has cracks down the walls, but if any bits of paintwork fall down it will give The Impostor some more DIY to do when he's sniffing around.

I notice old Mrs Skinner next door peering round her net curtains. As the house is a semi-detached she's probably heard the shouting even without putting a glass up to the wall. I give her a *What do you think you're looking at, you nosy old harpy?* look.

As I turn to go down the steps I realize that although Snooping Skinner might have been looking out because of the yelling, she's probably also staring at the blue blanket I'm trailing from my backside.

Chapter Six

This storming out of the house lark isn't all it's cracked up to be, even if you do manage to do it without a blanket hanging from your butt.

It's all very well making the dramatic gesture of sweeping out and slamming the door, but it now means that not only am I wandering the streets without my moby and therefore unable to tell Sorrel and Lucy what's been going on, but I've also forgotten my keys, so that at some point I'm going to have to ring the doorbell and get Mad Mum to let me in.

The timing of this is going to take careful planning.

If I go back too soon then the grand strop will have lost its impact and there'll just be another telling off and unbearable tension all evening. On the other hand, if I go back too late, Mum will be even more furious. And if I stay out all night, then she'll almost certainly be furious *and* call the police, who'll call Dad, and then both Mum *and* Dad will be nuclear mad.

I briefly toy with the thought that this might be a good idea after all, as perhaps they would end up at the police station *together*, and as the detectives were interviewing them about my disappearance over plastic cups of strong sugary tea they'd realize how much they missed each other and get back together.

I quickly abandon that plan as however much I want the parentals to reunite, I'm not sure I fancy a night on a park bench surrounded by smelly tramps passing around cans of strong lager, even if I do have my own bedding with me. No, I'll need to pick a time that's just long enough to prove my point, but not so long as to make things worse. Perhaps about an hour will do it.

As well as having no keys and no moby, I've got no money or my bus pass, so I just start wandering around the streets, killing time until I feel it's safe to go home.

I walk out of the bottom of Mortimer Road, turn left into Talbot Road, left again into Middle Drive, round Priory Gardens and then back to Talbot Road. I'm giving my road a wide berth, just in case Mum is lying in wait for me and grabs me by the ankles as I go past.

It's still light and warm and the smell of burning flesh is all around as people throw bits of meat on to barbecues in their back gardens. I wonder if Sorrel is walking around the streets where she lives, sniffing the air or maybe even just gatecrashing the odd barbie in the hope of someone giving her a burnt burger or a cremated sausage.

I'm just on another lap through Priory Gardens, wondering what veggies put on a barbecue, and whether putting a skewer through a carrot turns it into a carrot kebab, when I see three boys from school, Pinhead, Gibbo and Spud, sauntering towards me on the other side of the road, laughing their greasy little heads off. They look as if they've been up to no good, and I notice Spud and Gibbo have spray cans in their hand.

Just looking at them makes me realize how tragic and childish the boys at Burke's are compared to the KW talent.

Even though it's warm, Pinhead has got his hoodie up. I think he wears his hood up as often as possible to make his head look bigger, but it doesn't make any difference. He's still a six-foot beanpole with a pale little shrivelled head perched on top, and the constant hoodie-wearing makes him look like a teenage grim reaper.

I absolutely do *not* fancy any of them, and would be horrified if they even dared to throw a glance in my direction.

Jerks!

They *completely* ignored me as they went past, even though I tossed my hair, sucked in my belly and held the woolly throw over my mismatched boobs.

I'm pretty miffed that they blanked me. I mean, I don't want to have any interaction with them, but it's a bit tragic if even the school's losers don't so much as throw a furtive ogle in your direction. Even Spud has snubbed me! Spud, who being small, round, and pale with dodgy flaky skin wouldn't even get on to the bottom rung of my S-Scale. I've been rejected by the dross! The least I could have expected was one of them yelling, 'Can we read your meter, Lekky?' and then I could have given them a mouthful of abuse, but to be ignored by the lowest of the low is *totally* humiliating.

Ahead of me is a figure sitting on the kerb, hunched over.

As I get closer I see a podgy face and the outline of a weird beaky nose sticking out from under a lank greasy fringe.

It's the school's most unfortunate boy. The boy with multiple nicknames.

His real name is Frazer Burns, but of course everyone calls him Razor Burns, except me, Luce and Sorrel who call him Freak Boy or FB because he really is freaky the way he scuttles around like a beetle, all hunched over, reciting weird facts such as the population of China and how more people are killed by falling coconuts each year than are eaten by sharks. As if anyone is really interested or impressed.

Because of his puffin-shaped beaky nose he's also known as Beak Boy, and I've heard him called Alien Boy and Freaky Beaky Boy, oh, and Beetle Boy.

We don't call him any of these names to his face, of course, but others do. Maybe that's why he always keeps his head down and talks to himself. No one else will.

I'm thinking of crossing over to the other side of the road and wrapping my head in the blanket like criminals do when they're getting out of the police van to go to court, when FB looks up and sees me. Hopefully he'll pretend to ignore me. Even though I couldn't get a wolf whistle out of saddo Spud, Freak Boy wouldn't dare make the first move and speak to me. FB is the lowest of the low. Sub-Spud even.

'Electra? Can you help me? Please?'

I stand rooted to the pavement with shock and disgust. Not only has FB spoken to me, he's said my name in that awful squeaky testosterone-devoid voice of his. How dare Freak Boy interact with me first!

It's too late for the blanket-over-the-head routine. Perhaps I could just pretend I didn't hear him or see him.

By the time I've thought about whether a deaf and blind girl should be wandering the streets in the early evening without so much as a mobile phone and her bus pass, but with a blue blanket clamped to her gut, I'm level with the beaky alien and it's too late to turn back. He's rubbing his left ankle, and although he doesn't look up at me, I can tell he's been crying. The beaky nose looks so red it practically glows like a beacon in the middle of his podgy face. That's *another* name to add to the list. Beacon Boy.

'I think I might have broken my ankle,' FB gasps.

I don't want to get too close to him, so I peer at his feet from a safe impossible-to-accidentally-touch distance. He has no shoes or socks on either foot so I see his horrible skinny feet which are *huge*, like flippers with hairy toes stuck on the end. The sight of them makes me feel sick, especially when I see his ankle which is really swollen, like someone's blown it up with a bicycle pump.

From the end of the road comes the sound of jeering.

It's The Grim Reaper and his gang.

They're standing on the corner making *Tosser* gestures with their hands, doubled over with laughter.

I give them a finger back, not because they've been bullying Freak Boy, but because they dared to ignore me despite my best hair-tossing and stomach-sucking.

73

'Did those losers do this to you?' I ask, trying not to look directly at the bony flippers or catch FB's eye.

He's still rubbing his left ankle and wincing in pain.

'Sort of. I fell over trying to get my shoes.'

He looks up and I follow his gaze.

Dangling from a telephone wire strung across the road is a pair of black trainers. His white socks are hanging from a nearby tree.

'They took my shoes and socks off me, and when they went to throw them in the air, I tried to catch them and fell over. Now I can't walk.' Freak Boy looks embarrassed. 'Can you help me up and get me home? It's not far.'

I don't want to touch Freak Boy, but can I really be hard-hearted enough to leave an injured person stranded on the pavement?

'Can't you phone your mum or dad or someone?' I say, having decided that FB isn't a person, he's a Freak, and therefore it's not being bitchy to leave him on the side of the road to fend for himself. It's not as if he's dying.

He shakes his head. 'My phone broke in my back pocket when I fell over. There's no signal. Could I use yours?'

I can't believe I haven't got a phone on me!

When I first wanted one and Mum wasn't keen, I used to say, 'But it will only be for emergencies!' And now there is an emergency, I'm moby-less. Typical!

I should help him really. He helped me when I wanted to know the real reason why Dad left home. I never really bought into that whole *I'm having a mid-life crisis and I need time* excuse Dad gave, so I got FB to follow Dad on his mountain bike and prepare a sort of report about where he went. Because Dad kept going to the dentist's and had his teeth whitened we deduced he had crummy gnashers, completely missing it was because he was sleeping with his dental hygienist.

I look down at FB hunched on the pavement, rubbing his puffy ankle. Just because he acted as a teenage private detective six months ago doesn't mean I owe him anything, but still . . .

'I've come out without my moby,' I say, dragging him up by his elbow. 'Come on, let's get you home.'

Even though Compton Avenue is only the other side of Talbot Road it's taking *ages* to get anywhere, and I'm hot and bothered and freaked that someone I know will see me. I've got the blanket thrown over my right shoulder whilst FB leans on my left one and hops along on his right foot. Every so often he'll try to put his left foot down to test it out, and then give a sort of high-pitched groan, which *really* irritates me as it's just drawing attention to the fact that I'm with a hopping alien.

'ARGH!'

This is more than a groan. It's moved up several pain notches into the yelling category.

'Now what?' I say, sounding rather snappier than I meant to.

'I've hurt my foot!' FB moans.

'I know that!' I want to slap him but I don't want my hand to get anywhere near his podgy face. 'Why do you think we're both hobbling along like hunchbacks?'

'No. I mean I've hurt my good foot. I think I must have stepped on some broken glass or something.'

He's holding on to my shoulder, hopping from one leg to another like a demented flamingo.

'Hey, dude! You OK?' asks a low gravelly voice behind us.

I swivel my head, and there, standing next to me with the evening sun setting behind him is The Spanish Lurve God dressed in a white T-shirt. Well, not just a white T-shirt. That would be weird. Exciting, but weird. He's holding on to his bike and looking Spanish and smouldering and *totally* gorge.

I can't believe it! In the past whenever there's been the *slightest* chance of me seeing him I've made sure I've had clean hair, just the right amount of slap and suitably trendy but casual *Oh, this old thing!* type clothes. And now here he is, standing next to me, whilst I'm still dressed in grass-stained, juice-splashed and snot-speckled school uniform, a woolly blanket round my shoulders and my armpits radiating BO, whilst holding on to the world's most unfortunate boy who's moaning, has two mangled flippers for feet and is still jumping around as if he's standing on hot coals.

In horror at the situation I find myself in, I move away from Freak Boy just as he's in mid-hop, so that he crumples to the ground in a groaning heap.

Jags throws his bike on to the pavement and crouches down to look at FB's filthy flippers.

I'm tempted to ram my foot on to the nearest sharp object so that The Spanish Lurve God will crouch down at my feet too, but then I remember that I haven't done a pedicure for ages, and I've used dark-red polish and no base coat for months so my toenails look manky and yellow, and he might think I've got nicotine-stained feet. On the other hand, Jags might be *seriously* impressed by a girl who could smoke by holding a ciggie between her toes. I bet that's something Tits Out can't do.

'Listen, dude, that looks nasty. Do you want me to ring for an ambulance?'

FB's obviously in pain, but shakes his head. 'No, thanks. But can I use your phone to ring my parents?

Mum's a doctor and our house is only round the corner.'

'Dude, that's like *so* weird,' Jags says, handing Freak Boy his phone. 'My dad's a doctor too!'

I'm just about to gabble *I know!* when I manage to stop myself. There's no need for Jags to know I've Internet-stalked his family and found out his dad is originally from Seville, is a top orthopaedic surgeon specializing in replacing hip and knee joints and enjoys playing golf in his spare time, although even if I did say it, I doubt Jags would even notice. He doesn't talk to me. He just stands around whilst FB phones his dad.

I notice Jags is wearing a couple of leather stringy bracelet things on his perfect right wrist. I'd die of delight if he gave me one. A stringy leather thing is *definitely* worth several trophy ties, and Tits Out would be green with envy.

Within moments a car comes tearing along the street, screeches to a halt and a tall and totally gorgeous man jumps out.

It's Hot Dad, Freak Boy's father.

When I first saw Mr Burns, months ago, I gave him a straight 4.0 on the Snogability Scale, assuming of course that he wasn't married, I was much older or he was decades younger. But if anything he may have gone up a point or two in the last few months.

It's still unbelievable to me that this heavenly hunk can have passed his DNA on to the freaky beaky alien who's sitting groaning on the pavement. I still think FB was swapped at birth by mistake, or, possibly, adopted.

Hot Dad takes one look at FB's ankle and says, 'I'm running you straight to A&E. Your mum's on duty. She's going to get a shock when she sees me carrying you in.'

Jags and Hot Dad help Freak Boy into the back of the car, whilst I try and make myself useful, but I find I've got nothing to do other than hover around and pretend that the car door needs holding open, which sounds easy, but isn't if at the same time you're trying to suck your stomach in, stick your boobs out, cover up your shirt stains with a blanket whilst trying not to look like a refugee.

'Aren't you going with him?'

I realize that Jags is speaking directly to me.

The very fact that he's asked me a question turns my brain to jelly. I stand gripping the car door as Hot Dad climbs in the driver's seat.

'Your boyfriend?' Jags prompts. 'Shouldn't you go with him to the hospital?'

Oh. My. God.

Jags thinks that this weird freaky beaky alien with the flipper feet is my boyfriend. He actually thinks that I might go out with this aberration of human genetics. How horrific is that?

'We need to go!' Hot Dad calls out from the car.

I slam the passenger door *really* hard, and just to underline the fact that I am young, free, single and *very* available, I say in a loud and hopefully horrified-sounding voice, 'He's *so* not my boyfriend!'

As the car zooms off, Jags picks up his bike and looks straight at me with his gorgeous dark eyes framed by luscious long lashes. 'Don't I know you from somewhere?' he drawls.

For the first time *ever*, I'm faced with The Spanish Lurve God on my own.

This is my *big* chance to impress him.

I've been practising this moment in my imagination for *years*.

But which one of the many scenarios I've gone through in my mind shall I choose?

Shall I say, 'Yeah, I'm a friend of Claudia Barnes,' and therefore become sexy and slaggy by association?

What about tossing my hair and just murmuring, 'Oh, around,' in a mysterious sort of way, leaving him wondering where he has seen this vision of girl-next-door loveliness.

Or shall I go for the minimalist approach and just give

him an enigmatic Mona Lisa-type smile and look all coy with *Come Snog Me* eyes.

I do smile, but somehow my top lip becomes stuck to my front teeth and curls under. In a panic I toss my hair, but I can tell it's a jerk, not a toss. And then I say in a squeaky voice, 'I'm a friend of Lucy Malone. James Malone's kid sister.'

Chapter Seven

'He said *that* about me?'

Lucy looks absolutely horrified at what I've just told her.

It's a junk lunch day so obviously the cafeteria is packed with kids desperate to get their fix of empty calories and saturated fat, and we're in a long queue.

'Are you sure?'

'Defo, Luce,' I say. 'He defo said it.'

After I totally, utterly and *completely* humiliated myself in front of The Spanish Lurve God last night, Jags swung an admittedly rather stumpy leg over his bike and pedalled off, leaving me standing in the street in my splattered uniform, clutching my blue woolly blanket, feeling about two feet tall and two years old with my top lip still stuck to my teeth. But before he left he wolf-whistled and said, 'That Lucy Malone is one hot dudette.'

'I can't believe it!' Luce rolls her baby-blue eyes. 'This is *so* terrible. I'll never be able to walk around the house in my PJs *ever* again in case Jags is round and starts staring at me. He's gone from being James's friend to being a *total* lech. It's tragic!'

I can't believe that she finds being fancied by Jags something to stress about. If I looked like her I wouldn't be worrying about whether I was going to be caught in a pair of pyjamas with cartoon penguins on them. I'd be parading around in something small and slinky, flashing long brown legs and shapely arms. It's depressing to think that I could probably dance around starkers except for a couple of sequinned nipple tassels and Jags still wouldn't notice me. I'm obviously the opposite of a hot dudette. A freezing jerk.

'I think the fact that El Dwarfo uses words like dude and dudette is tragic,' says Sorrel. 'Not only is he a greasy-haired midget, he's a freakin' prat!'

'He's Spanish, remember,' I say, trying to stick up for Jags, even though he's given Claudia his tie, called my best friend hot and totally ignored me. 'And it's hair-gel, *not* grease.'

We're at the pile of trays, but Sorrel doesn't take one. On junk lunch days her mum makes her worthy packed lunches with things like rye bread and nut pâté sarnies, or wholemeal pittas stuffed with cold soya burgers and beansprouts, so of course Sorrel dumps the lentil food in the bin by the school gate and just nicks stuff off me and Luce.

I stick my plate out and ask the dinner lady for double chips and chicken nuggets to cheer myself up. I won't end up eating double portions. Sorrel will pinch at least half.

'Hiya!' Tits Out waves as we look around the hall for somewhere to sit.

She's sitting next to Butterface and Tammy Lennox-Hill.

'How come you got to the front of the queue?' I ask as I dump my tray on the table and park my bum on the seat next to her. At first I'm relieved to see she's not wearing Jags's tie, but then I notice it's looped round her waist. Cow.

She's rummaging in her bag and piling stuff on the table.

Amongst the gum wrappers, school books, pencil case, keys, bus pass, MP3 player, earphones, *heat*, Tampax and bulging make-up bag is a packet of condoms and a gold and white packet of Marlboro Lights.

I've never seen Claudia smoke and the packet of

condoms is *always* unopened, so I think she just does this displaying of slag accessories for effect, particularly when boys are around. Perhaps she likes them to know that if the occasion arises she's armed and ready, or maybe she just likes them to think that she's up for it.

She finds a Tippex pen and begins to touch up the white ends of her nails. She's always doing this. I think she has more Tippex on her nails than varnish.

'Some lads at the front of the queue let me in, and then I let Nat and Tam in,' she says.

Tammy Two-Names gives a sort of smug smile revealing a double row of silver braces. She obviously thinks that being friends with Tits Out is like being part of some exclusive sleazers' club to which she's now become a member.

Tammy isn't even a proper sleazer. She's a pseudo-sleazer who used to go by the name of Tamara when she was at Queen Beatrice's College for brainy snotty-nosed girls until her father's head cracked up last year. He had some high-powered job with a fantastic salary as Global Sales Manager for a drug company. Apparently one day he fled from a meeting, locked himself in the loo and wouldn't come out until they called the doc who passed tranquillizers and a bottle of water under the door. Anyway, I suppose you can't have a Global Sales Manager who won't even leave the toilet, let alone the country, so he lost his job.

The family couldn't afford the school fees for Tammy *and* her older brother Rupert, but as Rupe was about to take his GCSEs, Tam got the short straw and had to swap the grey blazer with the red piping which screams, *I'm minted, posh and bright*, for the green, *I'm just a Burke* one.

Of course Tammy didn't tell us this. She made out she'd been expelled for doing something totally wild and possibly illegal involving odd plants being grown in the school greenhouse, but then someone's mum knew Tammy's mum, and once the Mothers' Mafia found out, *everyone* found out about her nutcase dad.

When she first started at Burke's she tried to be a Goth, but all she could manage was wearing a black bra under her white shirt, and painting her little fingernails black. Then, last term, when the real Goths with odd piercings and strange straps on their shoes sussed her out as a lightweight wannabe with naturally dark hair, they started ignoring her. So this term she's trying to be a tart and has latched on to the Queen of Sleaze and her sub-sleazer sidekick. Maybe next year she'll take up hockey and try and get in with the sporty set, and her days of pseudo-slaggery will be behind her.

'So, what are you doing for your birthday?' Tits Out

asks, waving her hands around and blowing on them at the same time to try and dry the Tippex. 'It's next week, isn't it? Are you going to have a party?'

Lucy was fourteen last November and we all went skating, and Sorrel's birthday was just before Christmas and she didn't want to do anything but put a candle in a Double Whopper in Burger King.

Last year, for my thirteenth, Mum took me, Luce and Sorrel to London to spend my birthday money in the Temple of Style, aka Top Shop on Oxford Street, before going to see a film and then back to mine for a sleepover where we didn't sleep, we just gossiped and giggled and then felt shattered in the morning.

But before I get a chance to tell them that what with Mum and Dad being at war I haven't thought much about my birthday, Tammy butts in in that awful eager breathy staccato voice posh girls from Queen Bee's have. She might try to be a slaggy ex-Goth, but her accent gives her away as pure rich-bitch.

'Oh. Like. *So* cool. Like, you've just *so* like got to have a party. The parties we had at QB were, just, like, *so* fab. Jocasta Merry vomited, like, all night into the bath, even though Charlie Travers was already in it, starkers!'

Everyone giggles except Sorrel, who glares at Tammy and bites into one of my chicken nuggets in a *very* aggressive way. Sorrel and Tammy will *never* be friends.

'So, are you going to have a bash?'

Butterface has been swigging Coke but has suddenly sprung into life with this surprise question.

'Might do,' I say.

'Really?' Lucy asks, pushing chicken salad around her plate.

I'll explain to Luce and Sorrel later that there's *no way* on earth that I would have a party. If Mum was there it would really cramp my style as she still thinks parties should have jelly, ice cream and a magician with a rabbit, but if Mum wasn't there then I could see it turning into the sort of bash where the living-room furniture is rearranged in the back garden, shampoo's put in the fish pond (not that we have a pond but you know what I mean) and there are weird people I've never met making out under the kitchen table.

But I don't want to let the tarty trio know this, so I say casually, 'Yeah, if I can get rid of my mum for the weekend.'

'That reminds me. How's your plan going?' asks Tits Out.

For a moment I think she knows about my secret plan to marry Jags, but she must have seen the horrified look on my face as to my mega relief she says, 'To get your parents back together.'

'I don't think it's going to be as easy as I thought,' I say. 'I'm sure if they could just see each other they'd realize they miss each other, but Mum won't let him even put a toenail inside the front door.'

'So,' Tits Out says, stuffing her schoolwork and slaggy accessories back in her bag, 'set them up on a blind date. It'll either be fireworks or violins, but I'd bet on your mum firing a rocket up your dad's lying backside.'

'What's Old Teapot going to spout about now?' asks Sorrel as we file in to the school hall.

I'm gutted that we've had an announcement over the tannoy that afternoon break is cancelled as the headmaster wants to address the school. The *only* reason I managed to limp through English language and can face physics is the thought of twenty minutes' free time to eat a Flake and get some sun.

Mr Thomson stands on the stage at the front of school. He's short and stout and always has his right hand on his hip whilst he waves his left arm around which is why most of us call him The Teapot, though he's also known as The Tosspot.

'I've been contacted this morning by the father of a boy in Year 9. He tells me there was an incident in Priory

Gardens last night which resulted in his son being taken to hospital with a badly sprained ankle, a cut foot, a broken mobile phone and missing his shoes and socks.'

There's loads of sniggering in the hall, and Luce, Sorrel and I exchange knowing glances.

When I'd told them what had happened last night, my expert medical diagnosis based on watching lots of hospital dramas had been that Freak Boy had broken his left ankle in several places and would need surgery, and that his right foot was so badly cut he'd *definitely* need stitches. I'm now totally miffed that I'd gone to all that trouble of helping him walk and humiliating myself in front of Jags, when all that had been wrong with him was a common or garden sprained ankle, and a cut that a plaster would have covered.

'The staff at Flora Burke's Community School will not tolerate bullying in *any* form. If anyone knows anything about this incident they should either speak to me, tell your form teacher, or even write an anonymous letter.'

Old Teapot's eyes narrow as his left hand sweeps across the school hall.

'Does *anyone* know *anything*?'

There's lots of chattering and looking around.

There's no sign of Pinhead, Gibbo or Spud. They probably climbed over the gates the moment morning reg was over and won't climb back until the end of the day.

'We *will* find out who is responsible, and they *will* be punished!' There's a final flurry of arm-waving before The Teapot marches off the stage, followed by a row of grim-faced teachers including Buff Butler, whose butt looks particularly peachy in profile.

'Are you going to say something to Mr Thomson?' Lucy whispers as we file out at snails' pace, delaying our visit to the prison known as the science block.

'Er . . . planet earth to spaceship,' Sorrel hisses. 'Don't you think if Freak Boy wanted the school to know who it was who strung up his sneakers and bust his ankle he'd have told his old man? It's not like FB didn't know who did it.'

'But Mr Burns must know it was more than just an accident, otherwise why did he contact Mr Thomson?' Lucy says.

'FB won't have said anything for fear of a revenge attack, but Hot Dad will have put two and two together and come up with four,' I tell her.

Lucy looks confused, bless her. 'But two and two do make four. Don't they?'

'Yeah, but Freak Boy doesn't want his dad to know he's got the right answer,' says Sorrel. 'Otherwise he'd have named names.'

'And it's not as if they actually pushed him over,' I say. 'He fell, and anyway it's only a sprained ankle, not a proper injury.'

'So you're not going to say anything?' I can tell from Lucy's voice she doesn't approve. She has that slightly stern disappointed tone that her mum had when she discovered that Sorrel and I left blobs of chewing gum in the Beast Car, on purpose.

'FB wouldn't want us to stick our beaks into his business,' I say.

Lucy purses her lips in the way that Bella does. Maybe she really *is* turning into her mum. 'Well, whether he wants you to or not, *I* think you *should* be a sticky beak. He's being bullied and that's serious.'

Chapter Eight

I decide not to make a bad situation even worse, and head straight home after school. If Mum is nuclear mad at me, I doubt a day doing the housework has calmed her down.

After I did my impression of a dribbling rugrat in front of Jags last night, I had to go home and ring the doorbell to be faced with Mad Mum, dripping wet with white bubbles quivering on her shoulders, wearing only a pink towel and a yellow flowery bath hat. Not only was she mad at me for being rude to Phil, for lying to her, for calling her selfish, for stomping out and for staying out, she was mad at me for getting her out of the bath.

She screamed at me to go to my room, and then continued to scream at me as I was trying to get to my room, which is a loft conversion in the attic. The thing was, she was so mad, so out of control, that the screaming made no sense at all, so I've absolutely no idea what she was yelling, though I don't think I helped matters by shouting, 'All right! All right! Keep your flowery bath hat on!' as I ran past her.

Then, when I was in my room, I realized that my bag with my moby and iPod in it was still on the kitchen table, but I just didn't dare run past enemy lines in case I was ambushed by more yelling from the semi-naked bath-hatted Mad Mum. So I put on my Snoopy nightie, pulled the duvet over my head, and went over and over the whole Lurve God catastrophe until eventually I fell asleep hugging my pillow, only to have nightmares about being in a romper suit, in a pram, with a dummy rammed in my mouth, being pushed around the school playground by Luce and Jags.

Given that Mum's already nuclear mad at me, there's no point in winding her up even further, not before my birthday anyway. Once I've got the cash and pressies I can just go for it and not worry about the consequences.

Actually, after what Tits Out said at lunch I've been thinking about how I could combine my birthday with getting the parentals back together, and I'm beginning to formulate a plan which is so daring, so cunning and so completely and utterly fabulous, even I'm amazed at my brilliance. I'm going to call it Operation Bald Eagle and I'm pretty sure it's going to work.

I've just got off the bus and am walking towards Mortimer Road, running through the finer details of my master plan in my mind, when I hear the low hum of an engine near me and I'm aware that there's a car beside me, slowly moving along the road. As I walk a bit faster the car speeds up. As I slow down to a slug crawl, it slows down.

Oh. My. God!

I'm being kerb-crawled!

Some loser perv who's into schoolgirls in minging kilts and white shirts is trying to pick me up. At quarter past four on a summer's afternoon!

I can't decide whether it's best to:

A. Phone Sorrel and/or Lucy.

B. Turn and get the perv's number plate which I will then memorize for the police who will be amazed that I kept so cool whilst about to be kidnapped.

C. Rush up to the nearest house and beat on the door screaming, 'There's a weirdo on the loose! Let me in!'

I'm still debating my options when the car pulls ahead and stops. I look at it carefully in case I need to give evidence later. It's a sleek dark-blue BMW, probably top of the range and what Phil would describe as *fully loaded*.

The driver's door opens and a man jumps out.

Oh my God! I *am* about to be kidnapped!

But then I see the potential kidnapper. It's Hot Dad. Freak Boy's father. It's probably the same car as he was driving last night, but I was too busy trying to impress Jags to notice it was serious money on wheels.

'Hello!' Hot Dad flashes the most gorgeous smile. He's either been born perfect or has had *loads* of orthodontics. He leans across the roof of the car with a bronzed arm sticking out of the end of a crisp white shirt, and with that one movement adds another point to his Snogability Scale score. 'Sorry if I startled you. It's Electra, isn't it?'

I smile back in what I hope is a casual surprised sort of way, as if the thought of being bundled into a posh German car and driven off at top speed to a deserted warehouse in the middle of nowhere was the last thing on my mind.

'I'm Duncan Burns. Frazer's father? I think you were with him last night when he hurt his ankle?'

Uh oh. Interrogation by Dunc the Hunk. He looks concerned *and* gorgeous. A lethal combination, although I'm taking back the bonus point I gave him because I'm not keen on the name Duncan. Still, I'm going to have to be careful that I'm not so dazzled by his good looks I spill the bullying beans.

'He was already hurt when I saw him,' I say. 'I just found him sitting on the pavement.'

All this is true, so I'm not lying.

'So you didn't see how he came to lose his shoes?'

I shrug and find myself tossing my hair in a way that I hope shows off my dangly earrings at their face-lengthening best.

'Sorry, Mr Burns, I didn't.'

Again, this isn't a lie. I didn't actually see The Grim Reaper and his gang toss FB's trainers over the wire.

'And what about the other boy that was with him? The short, dark-haired one. Do you think he might have seen anything?'

'He arrived after me,' I say, wondering if perhaps I've been so blinded by Jags's fantastic good looks that I've overlooked just how stumpy he really is.

'This isn't the first time this sort of thing has happened,' says Dunc the Hot Dad Hunk. 'My wife Fiona and I are very worried, but we can't get anything out of Frazer. Isn't there *anything* you can tell me?'

'No, sorry, Mr Burns.'

To disguise the fact that this bit *is* a lie, I contemplate trying the shoulders-back, tits-out look Claudia does so well, but then remember the odd mouth and bug-eyed combo Luce says I pull. Also, I'm a bit shocked at myself for even *thinking* about sticking my chest out for FB's dad. He may be gorgeous, but compared to The Spanish Lurve God, he's well old!

'Never mind.' Hot Dad sounds disappointed. 'Thanks anyway.'

He's about to get back in the car when his head pops up again.

'Look, I'm sure Frazer would love to see you. We're keeping him off school for a few days, just until he gets used to his crutches.'

'OK. Tell him I might pop round.'

This is *such* a lie, but it seems the polite thing to say. I have no intention of going round to see his freaky beaky injured son and he'll know it.

'How about now?'

'Um . . .'

I need to think quickly but my brain has slowed down with all the lustful Jags and Hot Dad thoughts that have been racing through it.

'Come on. Jump in. I'm on my way home. I had an early morning meeting in the north, so now I'm skiving and not going back to the office!'

I really shouldn't get in the car with Dunc the Hunk for so many reasons, not least the fact that the parentals have always drummed it into me that you should *never* get into a car with a stranger, particularly a strange man. But Hot Dad isn't a stranger, he's gorgeous, the seats are cream leather, I've never been in a BMW and the journey to FB's posh detached house will only take two minutes. So despite knowing I shouldn't, I do.

'You have arrived at your destination,' says the satnav voice.

In truth, I'm very relieved when the car swings through the gate and scrunches up the long gravel drive to Freak Boy's house. The *moment* I got into the car, slammed the door and put the seat belt on, I realized that just because someone is totally gorge it doesn't prevent them from being a total perv, or that just because the car is swish and has air-conditioning doesn't mean the boot isn't stuffed with perv paraphernalia like rope and duct tape. As we pulled away I also realized that there was nothing to stop Hot Dad going the long way home whilst he put his hand on my knee or up my skirt. Flirting in my daydreams is quite different from doing it in real life, especially when it's someone's dad, so I put my school bag on my lap and sat with my hand hovering over my moby, just in case.

Hot Dad leads me round the side of the house into a fantastic garden with masses of perfect green lawn, and opens a door to a plant-filled conservatory built on to the back of the house.

Everything about the place screams money and good taste.

FB is lying on a dark-green sofa reading a copy of *Computer Weekly*, his left ankle in strapping perched on a pile of cushions, Archie the dog snoring beside him in the late afternoon sun. It's a peaceful scene.

'You've got a visitor!' announces Hot Dad, whereupon Archie starts barking and jumping up and down like a mental muppet dog, Dunc the Hunk shouts at Archie to be quiet, which just seems to send the dog even more loony, Glam Doc, FB's mum comes hurrying in from what looks like the kitchen to see what all the fuss is about, and when Freak Boy sees me I think he's going to leap to his feet with shock – probably not a good idea when you've got a busted ankle.

I say, 'No, thank you,' to Glam Doc's offer of a drink, and as Hot Dad drags away the yapping mutt, we're left alone, me and Freak Boy, together in an indoor jungle.

I don't sit down, but hover under a huge Swiss cheese plant so that FB knows I have no intention of staying long.

'Why are you here?' he squeaks.

Even though Freak Boy gives me the creeps, I can

hardly say that the only reason I came round was because I wanted to sit in leather seats next to a good-looking man in a swish car, so I say, 'Your dad saw me in the street and asked me if I'd seen anything last night. He must have rung the school. There was an assembly and old Teapot wanted info on your accident.'

'You haven't said anything to Mr Thomson, have you?'

FB rarely looks up, he always walks around with his eyes downcast and his shoulders hunched, but now he's looking at me with wide frightened eyes. They're quite nice eyes actually. Green. If you could take away the rest of Freak Boy's features and just kept his eyes, he'd be OK, although on second thoughts, someone with no face, just a neck and a couple of green eyes popping out on stalks would be even more freaky, not to mention the fact that the lack of a nose and mouth might cause severe medical problems.

'Did you?' Freak Boy's voice jolts me out of my freaky-body thoughts. 'Did you tell Mr Thomson anything?'

'Do you want me to?'

FB shakes his head. 'No! It'll just make things ten times worse.'

'That's what I thought,' I say, thinking that I'll ring Lucy the *moment* I'm out of Freak Boy's house and tell her that I was right not to be a sticky beak after all. 'But your dad knows *something's* going on. He really pumped me for info.'

'And you're sure you didn't tell him *anything*?'

More scared rabbit-caught-in-the-headlights-type green eyes.

I shake my head and look through the door leading from the conservatory into the kitchen where I can see Hot Dad and Glam Doc standing chatting. They keep glancing in our direction. I'm sure Hot Dad will be saying to his wife, 'Listen, the only way I could get a girl to visit Frazer was to practically kidnap her. It had to be done!'

'I don't know why you go to Burke's anyway,' I say. 'I would have thought your parents could have afforded to send you somewhere *loads* better.'

FB fiddles with the bandage around his ankle. 'It's Dad's old school. He doesn't realize how rough it's got since he went there.'

'But if you told him about Pinhead and the others he'd move you,' I say. 'What's the point of keeping quiet?'

FB shrugs. 'I expect I'd be picked on wherever I went so I might as well stay there, at least until the sixth form. Dad says I'm just like him when he was my age and he's done OK.'

I'm gobsmacked. Can it *really* be true that Freak Boy might morph into Hot Dad when he's older?

I've only ever seen FB smile once, and I was shocked that despite the freaky beaky looks, weird personality and odd beetle-scuttle walk, for a nanosecond the Burns genetic blueprint shone through. For that infinitesimal slice of time, even *I* could see that FB might have long-term potential. This has caused me no end of grief, as sometimes when I'm daydreaming about snogging Jags, Jags turns into Hot Dad who then morphs into Freak Boy and the daydream becomes a nightmare. It's something I've kept to myself, not even telling the girls. To admit to even vague lustful thoughts about Freak Boy would be shameful. But if Freak Boy's dad *was* a freaky beaky saddo alien at fourteen, perhaps there's hope of a normal life and lots of money for FB after all. Sadly, though, I'm not prepared to wait around for more than twenty years to find out, especially as by then I intend to be married to Jags.

'What does your dad actually do?' I ask, looking around, wanting to add, *to be this minted.*

'He runs a computer software company. He supplied the computer suite at school with all the programmes. Mr Thomson used to be his IT teacher before he became the headmaster. It's another reason Dad sent me there.'

'Even so,' I say. 'Burke's is totally crappola.'

'Then why do you go there?' FB retorts.

I snort at such a ridiculous question. 'Because despite the fact my parents landed me with a name which is supposed to mean *The Bright One*, I'm too dim to get in anywhere else.'

'It's not that you're not bright, it's just you can't be bothered,' Freak Boy says.

I'm not sure whether to be miffed that he sounds like the parentals when they bang on about my school reports, or secretly thrilled that he thinks I'm not a dreggy dumbo after all.

There's a long, awkward silence. I try to fill it by asking after his ankle and telling him that it was Jags who stopped to help him, but we seem to have run out of things to say, so I stop hovering under the foliage and head towards the door.

I say goodbye to Freak Boy, pass through the fantastic kitchen (all sparkly granite, chrome appliances and sleek cherry units), say, 'Thank you for having me,' to Hot Dad and Glam Doc, decline Hot Dad's offer of a lift home, pat their dog Archie, and crunch back down the gravel drive.

I know that Freak Boy is weird and picked on at school and no one wants to be his friend and he's probably lonely, but as I get to the gates I look back at the house and feel a huge gut-wrenching stab of jealousy which almost takes my breath away.

Not because FB lives in the sort of house I can only dream of, or because he has a dog and I'd *so* like a pupster, or because his dad has a swish car instead of a plumber's van and his mum is a doc and is glam whereas mine isn't either of those things, but because he has something I'm wondering whether I'll ever have again.

His parents are still together.

Chapter Nine

'Get off it! I need it to do my homework.'

'Tough titty!'

The front room is filled with the sound of things firing and exploding as The Little Runt carries on playing a computer game.

This used to be the living room, but as the kitchen downstairs has a sofa and a telly in it, as well as being near the biscuit tin and the fridge, we haven't used the front room as a living room for years. Instead, everything that doesn't have a home, or anything that we can't be bothered to put away (just about everything) gets dumped in here, either on the floor or on the sofa bed. There's old toys, a basket of unironed clothes which has been there so long I think we've grown out of them, books, a mountain of coats, piles of magazines, wellies still coated with mud, dust everywhere and just *stuff*.

We're not a tidy family.

Whereas Bella Malone is The Neat Freak, Mum is definitely Queen of the Grubs, and both Jack and I have inherited her chaos and clutter gene. His room is practically toxic, and even Mum calls mine the *Sty in the Sky*, there's so much stuff draped on every surface. When the floor gets so covered in clothes even I can't see the strips of laminate underneath, I kick stuff under the bed to clear a space. Bella Malone would have a fit if she could see it.

'I said, get off it!'

I try to pull the chair away from the desk, but Jack hangs on to the mouse, so as he falls off the chair, the mouse follows him, its wire dragging most of the computer tower with it.

Luckily, although Jack falls on the floor with a thud, the computer lands on the chair.

'Now look what you've done!' I yell. 'If this is broken and I can't do my homework and I get into trouble at school, I'll put a curse on Arsenal so that they all get food poisoning just before they play Chelsea!'

I give him a kick whilst he's still on the floor, which gets him up, but sends him rushing out of the room crying and screaming.

I put the computer back together, fire up the

email, and start typing, but just with the very tips of my fingers as the keyboard feels sticky and there are suspicious brown smears on the space bar. Jack has probably had chocolate on his fingers, or at least I hope that it's chocolate . . .

To: Dad
From: SOnotagreekgirl1
Date: 28th June
Subject: My Birthday

Hi Dad,

Mum's going out with Phil on my birthday, just as a friend tho. Can you believe it? Anyway, I'd really like it if just you me and Jack went out for something to eat at the Harvester, the one Uncle Richard took us to when he visited? How about 7:30? Mum will drop us off on the way out with Phil.

Love Electra xxx

PS I've had to push Jack off the dinosaur computer to write this.

I thought I'd throw in the bit about Jack and the old computer as a hint I'd like a chunk of top-of-the-range technology for my birthday, but the rest is a complete lie.

Mum isn't going out with Phil on my birthday, in fact,

I'm pretty sure Phil hasn't been round since I forced him out, otherwise he'd have fixed the hole in the garden fence which has appeared because Jack has been playing football against it.

Stage One of my Beat The Impostor plan seems to have worked.

For Stage Two, all I need to do is get Mum and Dad in the same room, which is where Operation Bald Eagle comes in. I just know if they met each other in a happy family setting they'd realize that despite Candy and the lies, they were meant to be with each other. For ever.

I'm pressing *Send* when Mum says, 'Jack's crying his eyes out in his room.' She pokes her head round the door. 'He said you kicked him.'

She's dangerously close to the computer, so I frantically try to minimize the screen in case she sees my email. I'm in such a rush, I panic and hit the *Off* button without shutting down properly. It's going to be a pig of a problem to get the thing started up again without it running through hundreds of error messages.

'He's lying!' I lie. 'I didn't kick him. I just pointed at him with my foot. And anyway, I needed the computer for homework and he was playing crappy games.'

'Well, let him know when you're done so he can finish his game,' Mum says. 'Chicken Kiev or lasagne for tea?'

'Don't mind.'

'Chicken then,' she says, disappearing.

There never was any homework, well, there is, but I'm not doing it now and I'll let The Little Runt deal with the error messages. I shout upstairs that the computer is free and follow Mum down to the kitchen.

She's got her head in the big chest freezer, digging out the Kievs. As her boobs are so large I'm always slightly worried that her centre of gravity will one day send her toppling into the freezer, and I'll come home from school and find her dead, stiff as a board amongst the frozen peas and Ben and Jerry's.

'You know it's my birthday next week?'

There's a cold and muffled, 'Mmm.'

She's bending so far in, I'm considering grabbing her ankles to be on the safe side. I don't want her freezing to death. Not before she's cooked tea anyway.

'Well, I was thinking. Maybe you, me and Jack could go out for a meal together? Maybe to the Harvester, you know, the one Uncle Richard took us to when he stayed?'

Mum emerges from the freezer with a battered cardboard box, flushed from having her head upside down in an igloo.

'Without Lucy and Sorrel?'

It will be the first birthday for years that I haven't done

something with the girls, but I can't invite Luce without Sorrel, and Sorrel would wreck the romantic atmosphere by staring daggers at Dad all evening, even if she was getting a free meat meal.

'Nah. I can do something with them the following weekend. I'd really like it to be just the three of us.'

'You do mean with *our* Jack?' Mum gives me a mega-suspicious look. 'Not some boy Jack you've just met?'

She probably can't believe that this is the same daughter who usually goes on about her birthday for *weeks*, likes everyone to make a fuss, and only a moment ago was beating the hell out of her little brother. I'm going to have to be *much* more convincing if Operation Bald Eagle is going to have any chance of working.

I go over and put my arms around her, just as she's putting the Kievs in the oven, so I get a huge blast of hot air straight in my face.

'Pleeeease, Mum. After everything that has gone on, what I want most in the world is just a quiet family birthday.'

And that's *so* not a lie.

Chapter Ten

Thursday July 5th.

My birthday.

The only day in the year – apart from Christmas Day – when I don't mind getting out of bed a bit earlier. There's nothing like a stack of presents and a wad of cash stuffed into cards to make you leap out from under the duvet and run downstairs in your nightie.

'Happy birthday, love!' Mum grabs me for a kiss as I hurtle into the kitchen towards the table.

Next to the Shreddies and the milk carton is a huge box wrapped in silver paper, a slightly smaller one in gold paper, a pile of cards and a brown airmail package

Jack comes into the kitchen, sliding across the tiles in his socks, holding a tiny present wrapped in tinfoil and waving a red envelope which he shoves in my face. I can tell it's been in his room as even the envelope smells of farts and stinky old football kit.

'Open it! Open it!' he says excitedly. 'It's from me and Google.'

The card is of a footballer scoring a goal. Not even a real-life footballing hunk I can assign a Snogability Scale score to, but some artist's dodgy impression of one.

'He chose it himself,' Mum says, winking at me from the sink.

Inside, it's practically stiff with Tippex. I hold it to the light and see that behind the *To Electra* Jack's printed on the thick layer of white goo, he'd originally written *Too Poo Head*.

'Thanks!' I say, trying to look pleased, even though the tinfoil package is a bottle of silver nail polish which I'll probably never use.

'Open your other pressies! Open your other pressies!' Jack is jumping up and down, pushing the boxes towards me.

Naturally I start with the biggest. The silver package.

'That's from Grandma and Granddad. Maybe you want to start with the one from me, the gold one?' Mum suggests, but too late, I'm scrabbling at the package and ripping off the paper like a demented puppy.

Inside is a computer printer. I think Grandma and Granddad S must have a *thing* about printers as they bought me one at Christmas to go with my digi camera. It does mean however that the big gold box might be . . . lots more scrabbling . . .

Yes!

It's a laptop!

I haven't opened the actual box but I can see what it is from the outside.

I'm *totally* thrilled! If we get the wireless thingy set up I'll be able to download stuff on to my iPod, Instant Message, get on wicked websites, play games and Internet-stalk people, all while pretending to Mum I'm upstairs in my room, doing my homework.

'Thank you *so* much!'

I rush over to give Mum a kiss, and then rush back to the table to open the cardboard box. But when I finally release the steely-grey rectangle from its nest of plastic and polystyrene and put it on my lap, I realize it's not so much a laptop as a thigh-crusher.

It weighs a ton.

Now, I'm no willowy weedling, but I can't see me being able to casually slip this monster into a bag and whizz around the place like they do in the adverts. I'd need a suitcase on wheels. But it's still my own computer and it means I'll need to find other reasons for threatening Jack with severe physical violence. If The Little Runt so much as lays a germ-infested finger on it, he'll be dead meat.

The brown package is a book from Jan, mum's friend in Australia who's also my godmother. I haven't seen her since I was about five, and the woman obviously thinks I'm stuck in some sort of infant time warp, as she's sent me a book on fairies. Punky fairies with attitude, but things with wings nevertheless.

There are cards from Grandma and Granddad S. Uncle Richard, Dad's brother who lives in Edinburgh, has sent me an HMV gift card. There's a big card with a Labrador puppy on the front from the American Wunderfamily, and Aunty Vicky has put a note in saying to order something off their Amazon account. The Impostor sent a card with *another* HMV gift card in it, but there was nothing from Nana Pat, who's usually good for some money.

The lack of hard cash is tragically disappointing. I might flog the HMV cards to Flyin' Brian for half their value, just to get some real money. Still, Dad will probably give me some. He's not really a present-buying sort of dad, so he'll probably go the easy but very welcome route of stuffing some notes into my hand.

Mum's flicking through the cards I've opened, putting them on the dresser.

'I see your father didn't get round to sending you a card.'

So my satellite-dish face doesn't give away any hint of my master plan, I keep my head down and pretend to examine the thigh-crusher's keyboard in forensic detail.

She doesn't need to know I got an early morning text from Dad wishing me happy birthday, and saying he'd see me and Jack later.

I'm back from school and sitting in my room peering into my little handbag mirror. I do have a big mirror, but I prefer to see myself in manageable bite-sized portions rather than face the full-on instant horror of the total package.

There are so many parts of me that I could stress over, but tonight it's my hair.

During Eng lit, I read in a magazine that a good way of disguising a round face is to *Create volume around the forehead area*, so I've spent half an hour fluffing up my fringe by attacking it with a comb, a brush, and half a can of solid-hold hairspray. And now I look like a poodle.

I've tried to wet it down, but my hair seems to have become water-repellent, probably because it's stiff with styling gunk.

Maybe it's time to ditch the fringe. I've been growing my hair to make my face look longer, but it now just hangs like a long, limp, mousy-brown curtain and the split ends are rampant. Mum doesn't know this yet, but I'm planning to dye it from dishwater-mouse-blonde to beach-babe-siren-blonde, but not in an obvious bright-yellow bottle-blonde way like Tits Out. I see myself as a classier less sleazy type of bottle blonde. Buttery chunks rather than yellow straw, and with less obvious roots. I was hoping for enough birthday money to get some professional highlights put into the mousy barnet, maybe even at Bella Malone's posh hairdresser, but now I might have to go down the cheap but potentially dangerous route of letting Lucy and Sorrel loose on my locks with a home highlighting kit. This is a bit of a worry, as a girl at school did her highlights at home and they went green in the swimming pool and then all her hair broke off. Not a good look, especially if you have a dish face to disguise.

I didn't mind going to school on my birthday, not if everyone else had to go. I didn't want to miss out on gossip and just sit around at home on my own watching losers argue on daytime telly. Ideally I'd have preferred not to go to school and for all my friends to have the day off too, like some sort of public holiday in my honour, but even I can't see the school ever allowing that.

So I had a good day despite a tough timetable and a *disastrous* French lesson where the Big Geordie tried to get me to say, *My name is Electra Brown and today is my birthday*, in French, in front of everyone.

I became all sweaty and tongue-tied and all I could manage was 'Je m'appelle Electra Brown . . .' before I got stuck and the Big G started yelling at me, not in French, but in Geordie, 'Ah howay man, Electra. Can ye not at least try?' which I think explains a lot about why I'm crap at the French lingo.

When I told the girls about Operation Bald Eagle, everyone except Lucy thought I was bonkers.

Claudia *Oh I know all about everything* Barnes reckons it's going to be a disaster, and has bet me a bottle of chavvy perfume that it'll be fireworks rather than violins. I accepted the bet because I'm pretty sure Mum and Dad won't have a row in a public place, on my birthday, when Jack and me are around. Mum will realize she still loves Dad, even if he has been a complete reptile, and who knows, Dad might even move back in by the weekend. What a birthday present that would be!

Talking of presents, I had some cool ones from the girls.

Lucy gave me a set of seven different-coloured knickers with days of the week on them, so I'm wearing Thursday under my black skinny jeans, with the earrings Sorrel gave me, a beautiful pair of silver dangly chains which are so long they practically touch my shoulders.

Claudia and Natalie gave me a black T-shirt with *IF YOU THINK I'M A BITCH YOU SHOULD MEET MY MUM* across the front in silver sparkly letters. Tammy Two-Names also signed the tag, but as I hardly know her, I think she's just a piggy-back gifter, the sort of person that never actually thinks of the present or buys it, but signs her name on the card and then shares in the gifting glory.

Angela Panteli gave me a string of purple butterflies made out of feathers which I've draped around my headboard, though I might have to think of somewhere else to put them as I'm worried the feathers will go up my nose and I'll inhale a fake butterfly in the night.

I think Freak Boy must have seen me with the presents as I've never mentioned my birthday, but when he saw me, he gave me a sort of head-down embarrassed half-smile and muttered, 'Happy birthday.' He also mentioned something about the 5th July being the anniversary of the bikini. I've got no idea what he was going on about, but as he limped along the corridor on his crutches, I was truly freaked that my butterfly brain conjured up an image of me looking all cute and slim-limbed, dancing around in a white bikini in front of Freak Boy and Hot Dad. Whichever you way look at it, father or son, it's a sick thought.

It didn't help that when we left school at the end of the

day, Dunc the Hunk was waiting outside the school gates in his Beamer, probably to make sure someone wasn't about to grab his son's crutches and throw them under the wheels of a passing lorry.

As I walked past the shimmering blue paintwork, I found myself tossing my hair and laughing, even though no one said anything remotely funny. In fact, thinking back, I was on my own at the time, so I probably just looked as if I was talking to myself and therefore certifiably insane.

I pull the birthday T-shirt out of my school bag.

It's true that Mum and I aren't really getting along at the moment, and I'm still not sure why. We used to get on, have a laugh, be nice to each other, but since Dad left home all we seem to do is lurch from one argument to the next. I used to think it was because Dad had gone and things had changed, but Luce says Bella sends her crazy and Sorrel can hardly bear to be in the same room as Yolanda, so maybe it's just one of those things.

I don't know how to get things back to how they were, but wearing the T-shirt is definitely not going to help matters, so I go for a white top, my skinny black jeans, sling on a wide silver belt so that there isn't too much pasty belly poking out, loop a string of black and silver beads round my neck, and dither over my choice of footwear before choosing some silver ballet pumps, which even though they look comfortable, give me excruciating heel-blisters.

I'm still having last-minute doubts about the poodle-head look, but it's time to go.

So that I can capture the happy family reunion, I open a drawer, grab my digi camera from its knicker nest (the only place I can hide it so that The Little Runt doesn't nick it) and go downstairs, where I stand in the hall yelling, 'Mum! Are you ready?'

'Coming!' she shouts from the basement, but I can still hear her pottering about the kitchen, opening this, closing that. It's typical of my luck that the Queen of the Grubs chooses *now* to start tidying up.

I look at my watch. It's getting tight for time. I've told Dad to meet me there at 7.30. If either he's early or we're late, Mum might spot his van, and then she'll be reversing back out into the road in a flash, and Operation Bald Eagle will crash and burn.

'Mu-um!'

Finally she appears from the kitchen, calls Jack in from the garden and starts hunting for her bag and the car keys.

I'm relieved to see she looks good. She's wearing a simple red and white flowery summer dress and the

Mighty Mammaries are packed into a reasonable bra, one that doesn't have them dangling round her waist or stuck out in front like a couple of watermelons. I hadn't dared tell her to doll herself up in case she got suspicious of my motives, but the thought of Dad seeing Mum in a purple velour tracksuit top straining at the zip from the pressure of the mega baps, a pair of stone-washed cropped jeans with an elasticated waistband and her hair in a pink velvet scrunchie had been a source of stress and a possible major weak point in my master plan. I only have one chance to get the parentals back together, and I don't want naff eighties hair accessories and dodgy sportswear to get in the way of future family happiness.

I take a deep breath as we step out into the street and head towards the car.

Operation Bald Eagle is well and truly underway.

Chapter Eleven

'Are you all right, love?' Mum asks, as I practically fall out of the car and lean against the silver bonnet taking in big gulps of air. 'You feeling car sick?'

I nod.

It might have only been a short journey but it's been a really stressy one, and for once it wasn't Mum's erratic driving that left me feeling green. I had more important things to think about than whether the sudden bumping noise was normal in a Ford Focus, or whether there could be a dead cat lying in the road with our tyre marks across its tummy.

First I made the *terrible* mistake of mentioning to Mum that I was worried my fringe looked a bit poodley, so Jack has been chanting, 'Poo Head's a Poodle-Head, Poo Head's a Poodle-Head' *all* the way here. As he was strapped in the back and I was strapped in the front, I couldn't even beat him around the head with my bag. But I will later.

Then I began to feel so nervous about the whole Operation Bald Eagle plan that I felt sick, but daren't get Mum to pull over because we hadn't time for a vomit stop. I just wound down the window which sent my hair into my lip gloss, and then a bug flew into my eye which made it water and smudged my mascara.

Finally I made myself really dizzy by holding my breath in case Dad's van was already in the car park.

But it isn't.

Yet.

I still feel light-headed and my legs are wobbly as we walk into the restaurant, so I'm glad that I went for the uncomfortable silver flats rather than the uncomfortable silver heels, otherwise I'd be swaying around like a newborn baby giraffe.

'Welcome to this Harvester bar and grill,' trills a chirpy waitress with a name badge saying *Sue* as we stand at the *Please Wait to be Seated* sign, just inside the door. 'Have you been to a Harvester before or do you need me to explain how the salad cart works?'

'Yes and no,' Mum says above the piped music.

'Lovely!' says Chirpy Sue. 'And how many is it for?'

'Three,' Mum smiles.

I'm not worried about numbers. I've already thought of this. Although Mum *thinks* there are three of us, they always put three people at a table of four, so there's still room for Dad.

I'm just about to follow the little procession of Chirpy Sue, Mum and Jack across the restaurant, when I'm enveloped by a fug of stale cigarette smoke and a couple of bony arms are circling me. I'm being squeezed to death by a skeletal squid!

''appy birthday, Princess!'

'Nana!' I practically scream, not from delight but from shock.

Nana Pat wasn't part of my plan!

Mum still sees her as the enemy, as when Dad first left home he said he was staying with his mum in her council maisonette on the other side of town, except he wasn't, he was really staying with The Bitch Troll in the flat he'd bought, and even though Nana Pat knew, she kept quiet. It sounds complicated but it boils down to one thing. Mum can't stand Dad's mum.

'Your dad's just comin' in wiv the parcels. Hasn't your 'air gone and gotten long?' She pats my head and I can feel my poodle fringe crackle beneath her yellow nicotine-stained fingers.

I glance over at where Mum was about to sit down to see her striding back across the restaurant, granite-faced, boobs pointing forward, weaving through the tables, practically knocking over the salad cart in her haste to confront the enemy.

'Pat?' Mum's voice is so sharp it could cut stone.

'Oh 'ello, Ellie love,' Nana Pat rasps. 'I didn't realize you'd be 'ere as well.'

She goes to give Mum a kiss, but Mum takes a step back leaving Nana puckering up in mid-air.

'As well as what?' Mum asks, just as she spots Dad coming in carrying my presents.

Mum looks shocked and then mad.

Dad looks shocked and then nervous.

They look at each other, but not in the lovey-dovey way I'd been hoping for.

Then Nana Pat looks at them in a sort of *What's going to happen next?* type of way.

Then all three of them look at me, and not in a *Happy birthday, Electra* smiley sort of way either, more of a *What the hell do you think you're playing at, young lady?* sort of way.

I start wondering how much Claudia's bottle of chav perfume is going to set me back.

'I just wanted everyone together for my birthday!' I

whine, hoping that the odd tear might spring to my eyes for added effect. 'I just wanted a family birthday.'

I try and make my bottom lip quiver convincingly, but there are still bits of hair stuck to it, and I'm not sure that a hairy-glossy-lip-quiver adds anything to an already very tense situation.

'Er . . . how many now?' Not So Chirpy Sue asks. 'And does everyone still know about the salad cart?'

'We're going. Jack!' Mum calls across the restaurant.

The Little Runt can't hear us as he's put a rolled-up paper napkin in each ear as well as one in each nostril.

She storms over, grabs him by the arm and yanks him towards the exit, his spindly little legs dragging across the carpet.

Jack, surprised to see Dad, wrenches himself away from Mum's grip and launches himself into Dad's stomach.

Mum looks *furious* that Jack is so pleased to see Dad, and rips the napkins from his ears and nose.

'I knew nothing about this, Ellie, I promise,' Dad says, as Jack does a good impression of a limpet by clinging on to Dad's right thigh.

'Look,' says Nana Pat. 'Why don't we all just try an' get along, just for a couple of hours? It is Electra's birthday after all.'

At that moment a few tears *finally* roll down my cheeks. I'd been trying to think of really tragic things like not having Buff Butler teach me in Year 10, or Mum driving over the edge of a multi-storey car park by mistake, but there wasn't even the *slightest* sign of moisture until I thought of Jags going off with Claudia and then several tears plopped out. What with the bug-in-the-eye mascara mess, Nana Pat squashing my hair and now tear marks running through the bronzer, I must look minging, but sometimes a girl has to make sacrifices, and I can't imagine that Jags is likely to be hanging around a Harvester. The Garcias are probably more of a tapas-bar-in-town sort of family.

'Pleeease stay, Dad,' pleads Jack. 'Have some chippies with us!'

Nana doesn't wait for Mum to argue.

'Get us a table for five, will you, love?' she says to Sue, who by now has *completely* lost her chirp and is trying to calm down the hungry grumbling queue that's formed behind us. 'And let's park our bums. I'm gasping for a fake fag and a drink.'

We troop to a round table and sit down.

Everyone orders except Mum, who says she's not hungry and sits with her arms crossed, radiating evils.

'Fourteen!' Nana Pat says, beaming a yellow smile at

me. She's obviously not heard of smoker's toothpaste; either that, or her gnashers are stained beyond toothpaste repair. 'It only seems yesterday that you was born! Your Granddad Kevin would 'ave been so proud of you!'

Dad's dad, Kevin, died just after I was born. He was a builder and fell into a pit of wet concrete on a building site and drowned, something I found bizarrely fascinating when I was little.

Obviously so does Jack as he pipes up, 'Did Granddad Kevin have concrete up his nose when he died?'

'Jack!' Mum snaps.

'Or up his bum? Electra told me he was really heavy in his coffin because of all the concrete.'

'I did not!' I throw a bread roll at him. 'I told you he had to be chipped out of the concrete *before* they cremated him.'

I look round the table.

Operation Bald Eagle is going *horribly* wrong, and we haven't even had our first trip to the salad cart.

I'm not sure what the other diners in the Harvester must make of us.

We look an odd bunch.

We certainly don't look like a happy family celebrating a birthday.

A boy with a couple of chips up his nose, who's using a cherry tomato as a football and the salt and pepper pots as goalposts.

An old woman, who in between mouthfuls of gammon and swigs of whisky, sucks on one of those pretend cigarettes that people use when they need a nicotine fix but can't smoke.

A younger woman sitting with her arms folded across her massive chest, staring into space with a face like thunder, eating nothing, though one look at her figure can tell you she usually likes a good plateful.

A balding man who's making so many trips to the salad cart as a way of getting away from the table that his steak is going cold and is beginning to curl up at the edges.

And me, who's finished my scampi and chips and is now stressing that my constant dangly-earring-wearing will cause my earlobes to end up like Nana Pat's, so long and flappy she looks like Dumbo with thick gold hoops.

I'm desperate to open the presents everyone seems to have forgotten are piled beside the table.

Luckily, the person who comes to clear away our plates trips over the boxes which *finally* reminds everyone that they are here because it's *my* birthday.

'Happy birthday, Electra,' says Dad, picking up a

box wrapped in Christmas paper. 'Sorry, it was the only paper I had.'

I expect Mum was rolling her eyes at this admission of lack of appropriate gift-wrapping paraphernalia, but I'm too busy ripping open my pressie to notice.

'Dad! You shouldn't have!' I gasp when I see what's inside.

He laughs. 'Well, you're worth it. Happy birthday!'

It's totally gorge. Small. Silver. Thin. Light. Powerful. It's also another laptop.

'No, I mean really, you shouldn't have. Mum gave me one.'

Typical! You spend fourteen years waiting for your own computer and then two come along at once.

Mum's looking smug and Dad's looking disappointed and neither of them are looking as if they want to jump into each other's arms.

I can tell without looking that the other package from Nana Pat is a printer. Even the grandparentals are double-gifting.

'Well you might as well take yours back and get your daughter something else,' Mum says. 'She doesn't need two.'

'I'll have it!' Jack starts bouncing around in his seat.

'In your dreams!' I snap. There's absolutely *no way* The

Little Runt is going to have a designer laptop if I'm stuck with the thigh-crusher.

'It would make more sense for you to return yours,' Dad says to Mum. 'I got mine through the company so I can reclaim the VAT whereas you can't.'

'Is that so?' Mum's voice is thick with sarcasm. 'Since when has a fourteen-year-old been a legitimate business expense for a plumbing firm? I used to do the books, remember?'

'Well, unless you've recently bothered to get yourself a job,' Dad hisses across the table, 'it's still *my* money you're spending, so if I'm trying to save some of it, don't you think that's up to me?'

Mum's eyes are blazing and her face is so red it's clashing with the flowers on her dress. 'I think Her Majesty's Customs and Excise would be interested to hear that!' she snaps back.

'Oh you're so bitter, Ellie, aren't you?' Dad says. 'You'd do anything to get back at me. No wonder I left and never came back!'

'That's rich!' Mum screams, just low enough not to get us thrown out, but just loud enough to convince me that at any moment she might raise the volume to window-shattering levels. 'It was only a few weeks ago you wanted to crawl back!'

'I did not!' Dad snaps. 'What gave you that idea?'

They both look at me.

'You said it would be great,' I squeak at Dad. 'You said if you could turn back time . . .'

'If I could turn back time I'd never have married him in the first place!' Mum butts in. 'I should have listened to my mother. She always said you were a waste of space!'

'I meant nice as in, it would be nice to win the lottery but it's never going to happen!' Dad says.

'Stop it, you two!' Nana Pat yells at them. 'Can't *anyone* in this family be'ave for just a couple of hours?'

No one wants pudding, not even profiteroles, and I decide not to suggest we sing 'Happy Birthday'.

It's not a happy one.

It's been the worst birthday of my life.

What a prat I've been. I've upset everyone, I'm probably in deep trouble with Mum and Dad and, to cap it all, I definitely owe Tits Out a bottle of chav water.

We sit in terrible, awkward, humiliating silence, well, silence other than the sound of naff music, Nana Pat burping and Jack farting.

My moby vibrates.

I look into my bag and see I've got a text from Sorrel.

I pretend I've got to go to the loo, and by the time I'm

in the toilets, another text has come through, this time from Lucy. They both want to know how the master plan is going.

Sorrel has sent:

Is the Bald Eagle back with his mate?

Lucy's just says:

Going OK?

I send the same text back to both of them.

It's a Harvester Disaster

Chapter Twelve

As if life isn't hard enough, my body forgot that today isn't a school day so I woke up at 8 a.m. which is ridiculously early for a Saturday morning.

To make things even grimmer, even though I buried myself under my duvet, I couldn't get back to sleep for stressing about how my life is going spectacularly downhill.

Everyone seems angry with *everybody*.

Mum is obviously angry with me for trying to play the secret matchmaker, but I'm still mega-furious with her for being so rude to Dad and *completely* wrecking Operation Bald Eagle.

Dad's angry at me for trying to set him up on a blind date with his obviously now soon to be ex-wife, but I'm angry at Dad for inviting Nana Pat, as even though I really like her, my plan didn't stand a chance from the moment Mum saw her.

I'm angry that Dad took back the designer laptop and colour printer, and now I'm stuck with the thigh-crusher and Grandma and Granddad Stafford's printer which only does black and white and makes clanking sounds.

But most of all, I'm angry with myself for being such a jerk.

How could I have been so stupid as to think that I could get the parentals back together? What fantasy planet was I living on? I'd really convinced myself that the *only* thing keeping them apart was The Bitch Troll, and once she'd gone, everything would – could – be back to normal.

As we pulled out of the Harvester car park we turned left, and in the wing mirror I saw Dad turn right, and that was that. I knew that my parents would never *ever* get back together. And at that moment I didn't have to even try to turn on the waterworks: the flood gates opened all by themselves.

When we got back I stomped up to my room and stayed there with the Goo Goo Dolls on at top volume, *without* my earplugs, before Mum came up and screamed at me to turn the music down.

I went out without any breakfast on Friday morning, went to KFC with Sorrel after school and had some chips, bought the smallest bottle of Burberry perfume I could find for Claudia, mooched around the streets for a bit then came back and went straight to my room where I stayed all night. The really irritating thing was no one even tried to tempt me back downstairs with a tub of ice cream or the promise of a Flake. They just left me there to stew in my own misery.

This morning, with no school, my plan is to get up, get washed, get dressed, get breakfast and get out.

I've arranged to meet Luce and Sorrel in Burger King at Eastwood Circle at eleven. We'd decided to go shopping on the first Saturday after my birthday *ages* ago as I was sure I'd have a purse stuffed with cash but, as it is, I'll just have to go into New Look and the titchy Top Shop and try everything on without buying anything. Sorrel's older sister Jasmine has a Saturday job in New Look, and it will really hack her off if we try on loads of stuff and then just leave it for her to put back on the hangers. Sorrel hates her sis because they have to share a room with bunk beds and Jas is always threatening to tell Yolanda that Sorrel uses mouthwash to disguise the smell of meat. I don't like her because she's tall, gorgeous and is rather up her own pert backside.

When Dad took the super-duper laptop back he promised he'd get me something else. I'd rather have the cash, but I can't see him handing over hundreds of pounds, especially as it would have to come out of his pocket rather than the company's, so I've definitely lost out on the pressie front.

Life's not going well, but if I stay under this duvet for much longer I'll die from lack of oxygen.

Death by duvet. That would teach them all a lesson, I think to myself as I finally haul my bod out of bed.

'Good morning!'

I'm surprised to see Phil sitting at the table whilst Mum flits about the kitchen making him a coffee and opening a tin of shortbread biscuits.

I hadn't heard the doorbell.

Does he have his own key?

How long has he been here?

Did he sneak in last night whilst I was in my room, drowning my many sorrows with eardrum-blasting rock music?

Even more worryingly, has he been here all night? That's probably why Mum didn't even try and tempt me out of my room.

Typical! You drop your guard for a moment and The Impostor sneaks in behind your back.

I don't say anything to him, but make a big fuss over the fact that the Shreddies packet is empty and I'm not in the mood for Weetabix. Flouncing around over the lack of cereal choice is so lame, but I can't help it.

I get a strawberry Pop-Tart out and ram it into the toaster.

The dramatics of this is rather lost as the plug isn't in so it keeps popping back up, but eventually I sort out the electrical glitch and stand staring down into the glowing elements, trying not to breathe in burning crumb fumes.

'We've been talking, Electra,' Mum says. 'Phil's suggested we go away for the weekend. Maybe next weekend, if that's OK with you?'

I give what I hope is a derisive snort, which is *such* a stupid thing to do as now I've inhaled a lungful of cremated pastry which makes me cough.

How pathetic do they think I am? Offering me a mini-break just to get round me. As if I'm going to be won over by a couple of days at Center Parcs or a caravan with a chemical loo on a windy beach.

'Er . . . like I'm really going to go away for the weekend with you two! I don't think so!'

'No. We meant just the two of us. Me and Phil.'

'On The Hog,' Phil adds, just as the Pop-Tart springs up.

I'm *totally* shocked.

They didn't mean me! They had no intention of including me! How selfish is that? They could have at least asked me so then I could have said no. As it is I've said no, even though they didn't ask me. How humiliating!

I try to maintain a blank face so they think I don't care, even though I do, but it's difficult to look blank when you've been coughing and snorting burning carbohydrate, and your mum has just said she wants to go on a dirty weekend with her biker boyfriend.

The thought of my mother being zipped into tight motorbike leathers and roaring away is deeply distressing. If I worry about her falling into the freezer when she's rooting around for chicken Kievs, how will Phil manage to negotiate corners with her and her huge baps clinging on the back? Her chest will be like some sort of ready-inflated airbag.

'You can't,' I say, hoping that even if my face looks odd, my voice sounds blank and disinterested. 'You're not built for going on a bike. It'll be unstable. You'll fall off and get rampant gravel rash.'

'Phil's taken me round the block a few times and I haven't fallen off,' Mum says.

I'm doubly horrified that they've been practising swinging their legs over the bike when I've not been around to see it. Still, going around the local streets a few times isn't the same as spending the night away, not unless they've been stopping off behind the bus shelter for a swift snog amongst the cans and used condoms.

'You'll get bugs in your teeth as you go along,' I say. It's pathetic but it's all I can think of. A wasp in the gob would certainly stop any snogging, at least until the swelling had gone down.

Mum laughs. 'I'll be wearing a helmet!'

'Then you'll get helmet hair!' I'm pretty sure I'm sounding all pleady and needy rather than disinterested, but I'm *desperate* to put them off their romantic getaway. 'It'll be all flat and limp and the heat will make your scalp itch.'

Mum ignores my medical advice.

'We thought we'd go away just for the Saturday night to a country hotel not too far from here. Jack can stay at Daniel's.'

'And what about me?' It's a mega-whiney voice, but I don't care any more.

'I'm sure that Miriam Finkelstein would be delighted to have you, but I didn't think you'd want to stay there.' Mum knows full well that the thought of being near one runt boy is bad enough, but two is beyond the pale.

I roll my eyes and hold them for a second in mid-roll for added effect.

Mum tops up Phil's coffee. 'I thought you'd jump at the chance of staying with one of the girls.'

I weigh up the options.

It's either Lucy's house which is constantly patrolled by The Neat Police for evidence of a cup being put down without a coaster, or Sorrel's with the exfoliating loo paper, farting cat and bowls of maggots for tea.

It doesn't really matter where I stay: how am I going to spend a Saturday night knowing that Mum is officially getting it together with the tattooed stubbly biker?

'I'll make my own arrangements, thank you!' I say, flouncing out. 'Don't worry about me. As if you ever do.'

I just had to get out of the house and away from the cooing love birds, so I was at Eastwood Circle *way* before eleven which is why I'm crouching in WH Smith's reading *Hello!* magazine. I don't usually crouch, but I'd heard a sarky assistant say to someone, 'Are you going to buy that or just use us as a library?' and as I'm almost broke at the moment what with the lack of birthday cash and having to settle Claudia's bet, I need to browse rather than buy, so I'm trying to keep a low, *very* low, profile.

My knees are aching and I think I'm going to have to stand up very soon when I get a whiff of a familiar smell.

At first I can't think where I've smelt it before, but then it comes back to me. It was the pongy aftershave Dad started wearing just before he left home. And then I look up, straight into the shaved armpits of Candy Baxter reading a copy of *Ideal Home*. The sad heartbroken cow is obviously wearing his aftershave!

What do I do now? I daren't stand up as she's directly above me. If I do, she'll see me. But I can't stay down here much longer. I think my knees are going to go into spasm, plus she could be in here for *hours*. The assistants don't tell adults off for reading the magazines, they only target the kids, which is *such* a shame as I could really do with her being asked to leave the shop *right now*.

I decide that the only way out is for me to do a sort of sideways scuttle, like a crab in wedge sandals, and then when I'm well clear of the gossip and *House Beautiful*-type mag section, perhaps at the far end by the car magazines, I'll stand up, ditch *Hello!* and make a dash for it.

But I find there's a reason crabs don't wear sandals, and it's not because they'd have to buy five pairs to fit ten feet. It's because a sideways scuttle in wedges is impossible and I've only done half a scuttle, possibly a scut, before I end up in a heap on the floor beside the kiddies' comics.

'Electra! Is that you?'

The Bitch Troll has spotted me and there's no escape.

She rushes over and pulls me to my feet, greeting me as if I'm a long-lost friend, not the teenage daughter of the man she shacked up with, even though he was still married.

'How lovely to see you!'

I try a sort of non-committal half-smile, half-nod look in the hope she gets the message that it's *not* lovely to see her, even if I have the satisfaction of knowing that Dad dumped her.

'Are you well?' she trills.

'Yep,' I say, brushing dust off my jeans.

We stand looking at each other, neither of us sure what to say next. The only thing we had in common was Dad, and without him she might as well be an alien in a pale-blue badly fitting sleeveless dress.

'And your dad. Is he well?'

'Yep.' I'm hoping that monosyllabic answers coupled with a blank face will give her the hint that I *so* don't want to talk to her.

Either my face isn't blank enough, or she's too daft to notice I'm really not interested in what she has to say, as she carries on twittering.

'I'm devastated that things didn't work out. I never thought it would end like that. Not after everything Rob and I had been through.'

I stare past her towards a shelf of computer magazines. Even stories about silicon chips are more interesting than this wittering woman.

'I miss him terribly but I've got my pride. I whitened his teeth and he broke my heart. I'm sorry, Electra, but your father has an eye for ladies and Caroline Cole was one woman too far for me.'

'Caroline?' I snap out of reading *How Many Hertz Is Too Many?* and stare at Candy. I've got a nasty feeling in the pit of my stomach. The same sort of feeling I get when I realize that I've revised for the wrong test at school, or worse, not revised at all. On the other hand, it could just be that her toxic aftershave fumes have finally got to me.

'Caroline Cole. The lawyer handling your father's divorce. He was seeing her behind my back so I walked out.'

'Electra, I'm *so* sorry.' Lucy reaches across the table and touches my arm. 'You must be gutted.'

I'd given the girls a run-down of my Saturday so far, and telling it wasn't any better than living it.

'About what?' I moan. 'About the fact that my dad lied and said *he* was the dumper when he was really the dumpee, because he's a serial womanizer despite being a slap-head with moobs, because my mum is about to start shagging an AA man with a death-head tattoo, because I had a rubbish birthday with no hard cash, or because my *entire* life feels like I'm drowning in a sea of crap?'

I throw myself across the table just to underline the fact that *everything* is going wrong, but sit up pretty quickly when I think of the unknown germs that could be swirling near my face.

'Don't be like that!' Lucy says. 'I thought you said you had a good birthday.'

'Duh, during the day! But not once Operation Bald Eagle got underway!'

Sorrel is working her way through a flame-grilled extra-large bacon double cheeseburger meal. She's probably had a bowl of rabbit food soaked in soya milk for breakfast, so I don't blame her for tucking into flesh. I'm having some Diddy Donuts because they're cheap and I'm hungry because I left the Pop-Tart in the toaster when I flounced out of the kitchen.

'I don't know why you're so surprised,' Sorrel says. 'My dad lied to my mum *loads* of times before they split up. He said one thing and did another.'

'You *always* say that and it's not the same thing at all!' I say, ramming a donut into the chocolate sauce. 'Your dad lied that he was a veggie when really he was a raving carnivore!'

'Listen, girlfriend. Lies is lies is lies,' Sorrel says. 'Whether it's about a bit of hot totty or a bit of hot bacon, it's still deception. Face it. We've both got Deceitful Dads.'

'So, where are you going to stay?' Lucy asks in the sort of way which means *Please don't say at ours.* I think she finds it really stressy being around The Neat Freak at the best of times, but it's doubly difficult for her when friends are round and she can't control whether we'll remember to use air freshener after going to the loo or plump up a cushion when we get off the sofa, all things which send Bella into a Neat Freak frenzy.

'You can stay at ours,' Sorrel suggests, 'if you've *really* nowhere else to go and can cope with the Loony Lentil lecturing you about how to hug a tree.'

It sounds to me as if neither of my bezzies are that keen on me staying at their house, which probably explains why they've stayed at mine like a hundred times more than I've stayed at theirs.

Luckily I have another cunning plan, and although my last one was a disaster, I'm sure that this one will go off without a hitch, even though I only thought of it on the bus on the way here.

'Thanks, but no need,' I say. 'I have a plan. I'm going to pretend to Mum that I'm staying at Lucy's, and then you two can tell your parents you're staying with me, and then we can stay up all night and watch DVDs and eat all the ice cream in the freezer! How brilliant is that?'

'I don't think Mum will let me stay at yours if your

mum isn't there,' says Lucy doubtfully. 'And I thought you were ditching making plans because they always seem to go wrong.'

'Duh, Luce! You're not going to tell her we're on our own and this plan can't fail,' I say.

'You mean you want us to lie?' Lucy looks all serious and worried at the thought of deceiving Bella.

'It's only a tiny white lie,' I say. 'More of a fib. Fibs don't count in the grand scheme of lying.'

'I'll be there,' says Sorrel, who's probably relieved I'm not going to have to share a room with her and snitchy Jasmine.

Suddenly she hisses, 'Hide!' and ducks under the table, dragging me with her even though I'm in mid-donut-dip.

Lucy's still up top going, 'What? Why? What's going on?'

'The enemy is entering!' hisses Sorrel, trying, too late, to drag Lucy down.

The girls had picked a seat in the window because they know I like to position myself in a prime Jags-spotting site, but this means that as well as spying on Spanish Lurve Gods, you can be seen by Suburban Sleazers, and within seconds I hear the shrill tones of the lesser-spotted common slag warbling, 'Hiya, you three!'

It's Tits Out.

I make a great fuss of pretending that I've dropped something which is why I'm scrabbling on the floor and Sorrel is helping me, and by the time we emerge Tits Out, Butterface and Tammy Two-Names are trying to squeeze on to our table.

'What are you guys up to?' Tits Out asks.

I see Tammy pinch one of Sorrel's chips. For a moment I think there might be a fight over the blatant daylight robbery of carbohydrate, but then Lucy pipes up, 'We're just planning a sleepover at Electra's next Saturday.'

'Like a sort of late birthday party?' asks Natalie, who's looking particularly pumpkin-faced today.

'*Not* a party,' I say firmly. 'Just a few friends over for DVDs and ice cream whilst my mum's away.'

'I'm in,' says Tits Out. 'What about you, Nat?'

To my horror, Butterface nods her orange head.

I don't want either of them there, but what can I say now? You're not invited even if you did give me a birthday present? I don't want you there because it'll mean I can't gossip about Jags? Butterface, can you bring your own sheets so you don't wipe your make-up on ours?

'Oh, like *so* cool!' Tammy Two-Names shrieks excitedly. 'The sleepovers at QB were more like scream-overs. It's totally brill your mum's away, Electra. Imogen's parents used to take sleeping tablets and wear earplugs just to get through the night.'

This is getting worse!

I can't tell Tammy she's not invited if I've sort-of-but-without-realizing-it invited Tits Out and Butterface. Perhaps Sorrel will tell them to bog off? But it's not Sorrel's sleepover and she's still guarding her chips from Tammy-attack like a vicious dog guarding its bone.

So all I end up saying is, 'Well, OK, but it's *so* not going to be a party!'

Chapter Thirteen

Mum glances at what really is an extra-large handbag stuffed with a couple of dirty T-shirts for added authenticity. 'That seems a very small bag for a night away.'

'I don't need much,' I say as she turns the car into a private road. 'We're going to spend the day trying on Lucy's clothes and then just blob about watching films this evening.'

This is clearly a lie. Lucy's a twig and I'm a salami, and Lucy's clothes wouldn't be able to cope having three times the flesh they were designed for being squeezed into them without mass seam-bursting, but Mum seems to swallow the porky pie.

She stops the car outside a large modern house called *Foxgloves* with a front lawn so green and neat, the grass looks as if it's been spray-painted on. Even the flowers look so perfect they seem fake. I can't imagine that any creepy-crawly gets within a metre of the house without being blasted into oblivion by Bella and her designer bug gun.

'I ought to just pop in and say hello to Bella,' Mum says, reaching to undo her seat belt.

'There's no need!' I say. 'Bella's out. It's just Lucy in this morning.'

I notice that the band of pale skin which used to show where Mum's wedding ring was has now blended into the rest of her finger. It's as if the ring was never there at all.

'And you're sure she's happy about you staying?' Mum asks. 'I really should have rung her to check.'

'Yes! Yes,' I flap, unclipping my belt.

Even though Bella is out at an antiques fair, and James and his dad play golf on Saturdays during the summer, I'm getting pretty anxious that a member of the Malone clan will turn up unexpectedly and give the game away.

I've spent all week stressing over whether I'm doing the right thing by lying. But Mum wouldn't let me stay on my own at Mortimer Road, and I can't face staying with Luce or Sorrel when I know The Lovebirds are shacked up in a country hotel, so really, I've got no choice but to lie, and as I said to Lucy, it's only a tiny-weeny very white lie, more of a fib really. I'm not lying about *what* I'm doing, only *where* I'm doing it.

'Well, have a lovely time. We'll be back tomorrow afternoon, but I'll keep my mobile switched on.'

'Thanks!' I say, trying to get out of the car as quickly as possible.

I'm thwarted in my speedy exit as one of the long dangly earrings Sorrel gave me for my birthday seems to have got caught up in the seat belt. I love the earrings, but I may have to sacrifice one to get out. Either that, or rip my left earlobe apart.

Mum turns off the ignition and swivels towards me. 'Look, I know this is hard for you, Electra, but after so much heartache, Phil really does make me happy.'

Oh ger-reat! The Queen of the Clams has chosen this moment to start doing the big heart-to-heart speech, just as I'm still fiddling with a trapped earring and need to make a dash for it.

'It's just when Phil and I decided to stay away from each other, you know, when you made it clear that you didn't like him being around, I missed him, and he missed me. It made us realize that we do want to try and give things a go. And then when I saw your dad the other night, I realized I'm more over him than I thought. So I rang Phil, and he suggested we went away sometime, and then we thought, why wait?'

I don't believe it! This is *all* my fault. My plan to get

The Impostor to leave has spectacularly backfired! Operation Bald Eagle *has* worked but with the wrong mating pair! I'm going to have to seriously think about ditching any future plans I make as they all seem to go spectacularly tits up, as Tits Out would say.

Now Mum's shell has opened, there's no stopping her.

'I know you thought you were doing the right thing on your birthday, and I'm sorry I was so angry. And I know you really wanted your dad and me to get back together, but it's too late. Too much has happened.' Mum gives a big sigh. 'You can't recapture the past, you can only look to the future.'

Oh, this just gets worse! Mum seems to have swallowed a self-help book, the stuff she's coming out with.

'Yeah, yeah, whatever,' I say, finally yanking the earring free, but making my earlobe sore in the process.

I scramble out of the car with a falsely cheery 'Byee!' to Mum and blow her a kiss as I do so. Then I ring the doorbell, and when Lucy lets me in, we both wait behind the front door and when the coast is clear we head back out towards the nearest bus stop, and take two buses back to Mortimer Road.

Chapter Fourteen

We're all set for the sleepover.

The iPod is downstairs and plugged into the speaker dock. I've cleared five cups and three cereal bowls from the floor of my room so that there's space for the airbeds. I've got sleeping bags out of the cupboard under the stairs, been to the shop and rented six DVDs, bought like a ton of Pringles, Cheese Puffs and Twiglets and several litres of cheap Coke, and I'm going to ring for pizzas later, but only if everyone will pay for their own.

'It's us!' Tits Out shouts through the letter box as the doorbell rings.

Claudia Barnes stands on my doorstep clutching several carrier bags, her chest thrust forward. It's grown alarmingly since she was at school yesterday. I think she must have double-filleted and stuffed two silicone things in each bra cup.

I look at the bulging carrier bags. She seems to have brought a lot of stuff for a one-night sleepover. Butterface and Tammy Two-Names are standing behind her also looking like pack-horses, but given the amount of make-up all three are wearing, the bags are probably packed with cleanser and cotton wool balls. Then they'll need all their make-up for tomorrow morning, straightening tongs and hair spray, as well as a change of clothes and underwear. No wonder they don't travel light.

'Go straight down to the basement,' I say as Tits Out squeezes past me.

She's wearing a tiny white top and a pair of jeans so low, they're not hipsters, they're more like bumsters. The low-slung jeans reveal she's wearing a thong with a bow at the back which makes her arse look as if it's been gift-wrapped.

But for once, I don't care.

After an afternoon of being pampered by the girls, tonight I'm holding my own in the *slightly-slaggy-chav-but-in-a-desirable-way* look. I've even managed to look at myself in my full-length mirror which is the first time for *ages*.

Luce gave me a pedicure (Crushed Plum), and a French manicure which looks fab as my nails are really long at the moment so the white tips are *massive*.

My hair looks pretty damn foxy too, if I say so myself. I think the hours that Sorrel has spent in the hairdresser having her hair relaxed or weaved or braided or whatever have certainly paid off, as she's used a highlighting kit from Superdrug and managed to give me sexy-messy blonde highlights without making me look like a badger. Of course my hair might eventually break off with all the peroxide, but as long as it holds out until school on Monday and everyone can see it, I'll be well pleased.

If only Jags could see me now he'd never be able to resist me. I'm all chandelier earrings framed by buttery streaky hair, with a padded bra on and wearing the T-shirt the tarty trio gave me for my birthday. The bra has just the right amount of va-va-voom so that the glittery letters really stick out. Because my chest looks bigger, my waist appears smaller, so the skinny jeans I'm wearing don't look as if I've poured myself into a couple of denim sausage skins and the silver high heels make my legs look endless. *And* I've no zits! Well, not mega-beacon ones so big they have their own postcode, just a few tiny ones on my chin which aren't yet pussy, so I've been able to cover them with a slick of Rimmel Hide the Blemish in Fair.

For the first time in my life I feel like a hot fox.

I *finally* feel like Electra the video vixen.

'Surprise!' Claudia opens one of the carrier bags.

Instead of a nightie and a toothbrush it's stuffed with coloured buzz juice, Bacardi Breezers and bottles of WKD, which she starts to pile on the kitchen table alongside the Twiglets and Cheese Puffs.

Butterface has a couple of bottles of red wine and lots of cans of cider, and Tammy Two-Names seems to have brought half a bottle of cooking sherry.

The stuff just keeps on coming and coming. It's like we're setting up an off-licence on the kitchen table.

I don't think I've ever seen so much booze in our house. Mum likes a glass of red wine or three so there's usually several bottles in the cupboard under the stairs, together with a really old bottle of Bailey's left over from the last time Grandma and Granddad Stafford stayed for Christmas, but there's no *serious* drink, which is why Nana Pat always used to bring a bottle of whisky in her handbag.

I feel freaked out about the amount of alcohol, but remind myself that just because it's there doesn't mean we have to drink it all. More of a worry is that they don't seem to even have brought one nightie between the three of them. Perhaps they're counting on borrowing one of mine? I'm not sure I want Claudia to snuggle into my Snoopy nightshirt. If she wears the double-fillet bra under it, she might pull the beagle's nose all out of shape.

The iPod is turned up to full blast.

Sorrel is sitting on the sofa sucking a Twiglet as if it's a savoury ciggie, staring daggers at Tammy who's swigging a Bacardi Breezer and wittering on about how she might go back to QB next year.

Lucy is trying to get Tits Out interested in the bowl of Cheese Puffs, even though Claudia is ignoring her, swaying and jiggling her bits in time to *Mr Brightside*.

I'm looking around the kitchen and wondering when to phone the pizza people when the doorbell rings. I'm not expecting anyone else, so I ignore it and start pouring Pringles into a bowl, but it goes on and on. Someone is keeping their finger on the bell.

'Hang on a minute!' I yell as I totter upstairs.

The constant bell-ringer is Mrs Skinner from next door, the wrinkly coffin-dodger who brings new meaning to the words Neighbourhood Watch.

'Hello, Electra,' she says, peering behind me into the hall. 'I thought your mother was going away tonight with her . . . er . . . new friend. She asked me to keep an eye on the house.'

Uh oh. I hadn't thought of the snooping Skinners! Mum dislikes them as much as I do so it hadn't occurred to me there'd be any contact between them. It's time to think quickly on my strappy silver-sandalled feet.

'Oh she was going to, Mrs S, but she didn't feel very well at the last minute.'

'But I saw her leave on a motorbike. At around 11.21 this morning. Wearing a yellow helmet and a black leather jacket.'

There's not much that gets past this woman. She's an über curtain twitcher.

'They had to turn back.'

'So she's here?'

I nod.

'Perhaps I could just see her?'

The old bat doesn't give up, but it's not out of concern, just rampant nosiness. Her turkey neck is craning so far past me into the hall, it's as if it's made of rubber.

'She's lying down,' I say. 'It's a migraine. She'll be in bed in the dark for *hours*.'

'Well, the loud music can't be helping her head, can it?'

I promise to turn the sound down, and Mrs Skinner retracts her rubber neck, gives up her interrogation of me, and shuffles down the steps in her slippers.

I go back downstairs and tell everyone that we'd better keep the noise down and draw the curtains even though it's still light, so as not to arouse nosy-neighbour suspicion.

After about another half an hour of snacks, swaying and swigging, the doorbell goes again.

'Don't answer it!' I say. 'It'll be the old harpy next door.'

'Or it might be James and Jags.'

I'm in mid-WKD swig when Claudia says this, and, in shock, I splutter, sending blue buzz juice down my chin and T-shirt. Lucy lets out a little shriek as if someone has stepped on her toe, and Sorrel just rams more Twiglets into her mouth.

'I mentioned to Jags and James that you were having a few friends round. I didn't think you'd mind.'

Before I can move, Claudia trots upstairs wiggling her gift-wrapped backside as Tammy adds, 'And like, I might have mentioned to some of the QB gang you were like, having a bash.'

I hear the front door open.

Above me it sounds as if an army is trooping into the hall as the house is filled with strange voices.

I start to feel really scared as people I've never met stream down the stairs into the kitchen and dump more alcohol on the table.

Cans of lager.

Huge plastic bottles of cider.

A litre of vodka.

Bottles of multicoloured buzz juice.

This isn't what I planned! I'd planned a night in with the girls talking about the S-Scale and teasing Luce about why she won't go out with anyone despite being a total dudette. What are all these unknown people doing in my house, and where is The Spanish Lurve God?

Through the crowd of strangers I see Claudia perched on the freezer, her chest pushed forward and her legs wrapped round the waist of a boy at *least* two years older than her with straggly hair brushing his shoulders and earrings in *both* ears. *She* didn't waste much time.

I elbow my way towards them.

'Claudia! Who are all these people?' I shout above the music. 'I didn't invite them!'

'Take a chill pill, girl!' says the unknown boy, circling Tits Out's waist with one scrawny arm whilst using the other to take a drag on a roll-up. He blows circles of sweet-smelling smoke into my face. 'It's supposed to be a goddam party!'

'It was *not* supposed to be a party and I didn't invite you!' I scream at earring boy. 'Who are you?'

'This is Buzzer and I can vouch for him,' Claudia says.

Buzzer stops smoking, throws the stub on the floor and starts to neck-suck Claudia who's looking over his shoulder in a way which suggests she might move on from Buzzer if someone better, like Jags, comes into the kitchen.

Upstairs it sounds as if a herd of squealing pigs has come through the front door. I wade past unknown bodies blocking the stairs, and make my way up to the hall, which is filled with screeching girls, all of whom seem to want to hug Tammy Two-Names.

'Oh – my – God, Tamara!' someone yells. 'How are you coping, slumming it with the Burke's chavs? I would just simply die!'

It's one thing to have uninvited testosterone flooding your house, but it's quite another having gatecrashing posh cows.

'What the hell do you think you're playing at, Tammy?' I yell above the noise, yanking her by the arm. 'Did I tell you to invite these people? Christ! I didn't even invite you! You invited yourself!'

A really snooty-looking girl pulls Tammy away and stands nose to nose with me.

'Listen, chav-girl. Don't speak to my friend like that. Who the hell do you think you are?' Her voice could cut glass and she has so much black stuff round her eyes, I'm not sure if it's make-up or if someone has already beaten me to it and punched her.

Before I can spit in her face and tell her that I'm the

owner, well, sort of owner of the house, I hear a car pull up outside and more unidentified people pour through the front door.

It's my not-really-a-party party, but I know hardly anybody. I drift around feeling like a stranger in my own home. I'm so seriously freaked about what is happening I'm wondering about phoning the police myself. Everything is getting out of control. I just don't seem to be able to stop the constant flow of people through the front door.

In the front room I see Lucy, clutching a bottle of Pepsi, talking to a boy I vaguely recognize as the ZBF boy from Pizza Hut. Butterface is sitting on the sofa on James Malone's lap surrounded by old copies of *heat* and a pile of ironing. Every time James puts his hand under her top Nat pulls it out, but it doesn't seem to stop him trying again and again.

'It's all getting out of hand!' I cry to Sorrel. She's sitting on the landing with a bottle of voddy, giving evil looks to the QB girls who are going into the bathroom five at a time, peeing en masse, probably in the bath as well as the loo. 'What am I going to do?'

'I'll lock the front door from the inside and guard it,' she says, wobbling to her feet. 'I won't let any more of those snobby cows in.'

She staggers off down the stairs, clutching the vodka bottle in one hand and holding on to the wall with the other.

I decide to go to my room whilst I think what to do next. If we can stop more people coming in then perhaps I won't have to phone the police after all. It's nearly midnight! Surely people will start to go home then?

I'm just at the top of the stairs when a figure steps out in front of my bedroom door.

'Great party, dude.'

I'm face to face with The Spanish Lurve God. An El Dwarfo Lurve God that stinks of lager and cigarettes, but still a Spanish Lurve God.

Actually, it's not quite face to face as Jags *is* a bit short and I've got my high heels on, so it's more my chin to his eyeballs.

'Th . . . th . . . thanks,' I stutter, though I'm not sure whether it's actually a stutter or a slur, as I've had more buzz juice than I intended to and much less to eat than I need, and suddenly I don't feel quite myself.

Jags hovers for a moment, swigging a can of lager. If he's not to head off to find someone who can string a sentence together, I've got to think of something interesting and witty to say. I'm not even sure if he realizes I'm a girl as he's called me a dude.

'You score 5 on my Snogability Scale.'

What!

I can't believe I've just said that!

I want to die.

Right here.

Right now.

That wasn't either interesting or witty. It was butt-clenchingly embarrassing.

'Have I snogged you?' Jags asks in his gravelly drawl.

Or maybe he doesn't drawl, maybe he's talking normally and I just can't hear normally. I'm certainly not speaking normally. The connection between my brain and my mouth seems to have gone crazy. Which might explain why I then say, 'Oh, not in real life, but we've snogged *loads* of times in my mind, and when I've practised on my arm.'

Someone! *Please!* Shoot me. *Now!*

Time for damage limitation if he's not to think he's talking to someone who's escaped from the local loony bin.

I see he's wearing a Rolling Stones T-shirt, so as a last-ditch attempt to appear interesting I blurt out, 'Are they like total rock gods or just wrinkly old muppets?'

'Who?'

'Them!'

I go to point at the writing across his chest, but the combination of alcohol, no food and high heels is a lethal one, and I find myself head-butting him whilst mumbling something even I don't recognize into his chest.

I think he tries to push me back, or maybe I try to stand up, but the outcome is that I feel myself sliding slowly down The Lurve God's body. In an attempt to stay upright, about halfway down I make a grab for something, *anything*, and manage to get a handful of material around the waistband area. But instead of stopping my slow and humiliating descent, I just pull his jeans down and land in a heap outside my bedroom door, my nose buried between his trainers, and something – his jeans? his boxer shorts? – draped on my head.

As Jags fiddles about my face, presumably to retrieve his clothing from around his ankles, I'm vaguely aware of the sound of glass breaking downstairs and then Lucy's voice crying, 'Electra! Come quickly! They're playing football in the kitchen.'

But after that . . .

'Piss off! Piss off!'

I come to to hear Sorrel yelling downstairs.

I try to get up but my head is pounding and the landing is spinning. My first thought is to get to my bed, but when I peer round the door there are a couple of figures in my room, on my bed, giggling. I tell them to get out, but they ignore me and carry on giggling.

I manage to slip out of my sandals and go down the stairs on my bum, bumpity-bump, to the next landing, and then more or less slide down from there straight into the hall, as if I'm sledging down the stairs but without a sledge.

From the sound of the music and the cheering as more glass breaks, I can hear the party is still in full swing in the kitchen.

'What's going on?' I whimper as someone continues to bang on the front door and ring the bell, whilst Sorrel screams abuse at them.

'They won't go away,' Sorrel yells at me. 'They're trying to force the door open. The chain is on but they're winning!'

Sorrel has her butt against the door but the people behind are pushing harder. Even Sorrel's ample backside is no match for a gang of alcohol-fuelled teenagers wanting to gatecrash a party.

'I'll tell them. I'll them to get lost or I'll stick a hot banana up their bum!' I'm sure I'm speaking but my voice sounds odd and I seem to be coming out with even more utter garbage.

I stagger to my feet, lurch towards the front door, and open it as far as the chain will let me.

'Want a hot banana stuck up your backside?' I yell through the gap. 'If not! Get lost!'

And then my eyes manage to focus, and I realize that standing on the doorstep, under the outside light, are Mum and Phil.

Chapter Fifteen

I'm dying.

Really dying.

The people in booze adverts don't look as if they're dying. They look as if they're having fun, smiling with their perfect white teeth as if they haven't a care in the world as long as they swig the latest buzz juice.

Liars!

I can't imagine feeling well enough to have fun *ever* again. My teeth feel as if they're coated in fur, I've got something crusty around my mouth which I'm pretty sure is dried puke, and it feels as if people wearing heavy boots are stamping on my head.

I try to move and another wave of *I'm going to puke NOW!* comes over me.

I barf into the bucket someone has helpfully put beside my bed, and lie back with an acid-filled mouth whilst I try to piece together what happened last night.

The more I remember, the more ill I feel, and the more I lurch for the bucket.

I remember Mum and Phil barging through the front door and there being lots of shouting and people being thrown out on to the street.

I remember Lucy crying and James shouting at someone, but I don't know how they got home.

I remember Mum and Phil carrying Sorrel to the car, and Phil driving off with her.

I remember Ethel and Frank Skinner standing in the hall squawking, 'Thank goodness we rang you! Thank goodness we rang you!' over and over again like a couple of demented geriatric parrots.

And even though I was barely able to stand, and focusing was difficult, I remember the absolute fury in Mum's eyes as she pushed past me at the front door and saw what was happening in her house.

I sort of understand why she was mad. I hate the thought that unknown bodies doing goodness knows what (but I can guess!) have been in my bed, and if I wasn't about to die I'd be up and stripping the sheets. Once Mum realizes none of this was my fault, she'll be OK.

The bedroom door flies open and I'm hit in the face by something wet and rubbery.

Then my bedroom curtains are drawn, the daylight floods in, and it feels as if someone is standing on my head grinding their stiletto heels into my eye sockets.

'Get those rubber gloves on and start cleaning the house.'

It's nuclear-mad Mum.

'Start with the bathroom. And get those down you.'

There's an explosion just near my head, and I squint to see Mum's banged a large glass of water beside my bed with two white tablets. Then another bomb goes off which must be my bedroom door closing.

Even sitting up in bed is hard. It seemed a good idea at the time to paint my bedroom walls Babe Pink and have a multicoloured swirly duvet, but now my room makes me feel as if I'm in some sort of drug-induced psychedelic nightmare.

I briefly toy with the idea that I feel like this because someone has spiked my drink or slipped something dodgy into the Cheese Puffs, but even I know it's only because I've OD'd on the buzz juice.

I take a swig of water to wash the paracetamol down, swing my legs over the edge of the bed and see I'm still wearing yesterday's clothes.

Oh, that's just great!

Mum is so *not* going to love the fact that she came

home to find her house trashed and her wasted daughter wearing a *My Mum's A Bitch* T-shirt.

I decide I might feel better if I have a shower, so I stand up really slowly, make my way down the stairs on wobbly legs, and go into the bathroom. It stinks of pee and from the look of the yellow splashes on the white enamel, the bath has been used as a second loo. At least no one's barfed in it.

I can't begin to clean up other people's body fluids whilst I still feel so rank, so I strip off, stick on a bath hat as I can't face the thought of rubbing my throbbing head with shampoo, turn the shower on and get in.

The hot water running down my bod feels fantastic, as if the nightmare of last night is being washed away. A squeeze of Mum's lemon shower gel also helps bring me round. But as I'm standing there I realize the water isn't running away. It's coming up my legs.

I look down to see I'm standing in a swirling soup of soap bubbles and puke. The plug hole is clogged and bits of sweetcorn, carrots and Twiglets are circling my ankles.

For someone so hung-over I manage to get out of the shower *very* speedily, but then start to retch again when I notice a piece of carrot wedged between my toes.

* * *

Getting dressed is mega complicated with a hangover. It's probably to do with not being able to look up, down, left or right without the room whirling around like I'm in the centre of some crazed vortex.

Eventually I manage to pull on some clothes, but when I go to the loo (which I clean by squirting a bottle of bleach around at arm's length and flushing it over and over again) I realize I've put on Tuesday's knickers, even though it's Sunday.

I can't face taking my jeans off just to change my undies. *It's not like anyone is going to see my knickers anyway*, I think to myself as I tie a towel around my face to stop me smelling the bleach and the puke, put the rubber gloves on and start to pick out the mixed vegetables from the shower tray. No one is even remotely interested in my pants.

I'm miffed that as far as I remember, despite there being lots of snogging going on in dark corners last night, no one tried to snog me. How tragic is that? Having a party, getting the house trashed, and not even getting a snog to show for it! Jags could at least have tried a peck on the cheek, just as a thank you for being a guest in my house, not that I think he realized who I was or even that he cared if he did. I was just the wasted girl on the landing who tried to pull his boxers down.

I feel sick, not just with the excess alcopops, puke and bleach combo, but with the thought I have totally humiliated myself in front of The Spanish Lurve God.

Again.

I can't find my trainers and I *have* to have them.

I can't wear flip-flops or sandals or anything else that might expose skin which could come in to contact with post-party vomit or worse.

Carefully, so as not to feel any more vomity, I sink to my knees and look under my bed. Amongst the piles of rubbish I see my trainers and a pair of sunglasses, but as I reach to get them my hand comes across something squishy, clammy and sticky. As I prise it from the laminate floor and pull it out covered in dust and hair, I realise it's a silicone chicken fillet. A single fake boob. The sort Tits Out uses.

Tits Out must have been in my bedroom!

I bury my nose in the bedding.

Now the bucket of barf has gone the smell of vomit isn't so bad and I can *definitely* sniff Burberry perfume on the top of the duvet, but thankfully not on the sheet.

Tits Out has been lying on my bed!

But who with?

The only people I remember near my room were the

couple I heard giggling in the bedroom which could have been Claudia and Buzzer. And then Jags who I found outside my bedroom door.

My blood runs cold.

Jags!

It has to be Jags! *That's* what he was doing outside my bedroom door! He'd been in my bedroom with Tits Out and I'd caught him leaving. She was bored of Buzzer on the freezer and had moved on to my fantasy boyfriend in my real bedroom.

The thought of Jags and Claudia in my room disgusts me and I don't know what to do next.

There's nothing for it but to try her chicken fillet on for size.

Mum and Phil are busy pushing lager cans into black bin bags when I finally pluck up the courage to go into the kitchen.

They look as trashed as I feel. I don't think they've been to bed which I suppose could be a good thing as it means they've not been to bed *together*, but a night without sleep probably hasn't helped their mood.

My legs feel wobbly. I'd like to collapse on the sofa but there's a nasty-looking wet patch on the cushions, so I sink on to a kitchen chair instead.

Even though I'm wearing dark glasses, inside, in a basement kitchen and squinting because I have the biggest headache known to man as the paracetamol isn't even nibbling at the edges of the pain, I can see that people have stubbed their cigarettes out on the pine table. It's studded with burn marks. There's a broken pane of glass in the back window, and someone, probably a Tottenham supporter, has stuck a screwdriver in Jack's prized Arsenal football so that it's sitting on the table, shrivelling in front of my bleary eyes.

When Phil and Mum see me, if looks could kill, by now I'd be lying on the kitchen floor, sparko, with my eyes rolled into the back of my head. At least if I was dead I wouldn't feel any pain, so it's not a bad option, under the circumstances.

From the stony looks on their tired faces I can tell they expect me to say something, a grovelling apology as to why they had to be called back from their love tryst to find the house had been taken over by teenage terrorists.

'It wasn't my fault, Mum! I *so* didn't invite any of those people. They just turned up! I don't know where they came from! I think they were mostly QB slags and KW boys!'

Hmm, I meant to say sorry, but it didn't quite come out as I intended.

'But why were you here in the first place?' Mum is practically hyperventilating with anger. Her chest is rising and falling so fast it's as if someone has stuck a bicycle pump into her boobs and is pumping away. 'You were supposed to be at the Malones!'

'I was, but then we decided to come here.'

The evils are radiating from Mum. Phil just looks shattered.

'Look, it was supposed to be just a sleepover, but I didn't know the others were going to tell everyone it was a party, did I?'

I wobble to the sink, find a mug that looks reasonably clean, and fill it with water. I feel as if I could drink an entire reservoir I'm so dehydrated.

Over the top of my mug I see Mum heading towards the phone.

'I'm going to ring that Bella Malone. I'm amazed she let you come back here knowing I was away. I mean, I know she likes to think of herself as a trendy-liberal sort of parent, but what was she thinking of? You're just kids!'

Uh oh.

'She didn't,' I say through watery gulps.

Mum looks daggers at me. 'She didn't *what*?'

'She didn't know you were away. I pretended to stay at Lucy's and Lucy pretended to her mum that you were here.' I take another gulp of water. 'Sorrel did the same.'

'So are you saying this was all planned? When I dropped you off yesterday morning you had no intention of staying at Lucy's?'

I shake my head which is a *really really* bad thing to do when you have a hangover as the room keeps spinning long after you've stopped moving your head. 'I came back here with Luce. Sorrel came later.'

Phil looks at his watch. 'Look, I could really do with a coffee. Tesco will be open by now. What do we need? Milk? Eggs? Bread? Bleach? More bin liners?'

'Oh, for God's sake Phil, just use your head,' Mum snaps at him, before yelling at me, 'Your so-called friends raided the fridge and there's nothing left.'

Phil goes and I try to follow him but Mum screams, 'Take these!' and throws a roll of bin liners at me. Luckily it doesn't hurt as it hits me in the right boob where I've tucked the chicken fillet to test it out. 'Now get out of my sight and start clearing up!'

I slink out of the kitchen with my roll of black bags.

I'm pretty miffed Mum hasn't noticed my new hair, but I guess she's got other things to think about and, to be honest, a night spent tossing around in an alcoholic sweat hasn't done much for the style. It's gone from sexy-messy to sweaty-messy, not a good look, especially as the ends smell of vomit and dodgy cigarette smoke.

It's not just my hair that smells rank either. The house stinks of booze, barf, cigarettes and cheap perfume.

There are cans and bottles *everywhere*, all empty. There are so many stubbed-out cigarettes on the piles of paperwork in the front room, I'm amazed 14 Mortimer Road didn't become The Towering Inferno. There's ash all over the green Axminster in the hall, and red wine up the magnolia walls. Even in Jack's room I find empty cans and cigarette butts nestling amongst his dinosaur duvet.

Someone has had a violent game of table football as the red-team goalie seems to have been decapitated. I hunt around and find the head on the floor. I might be able to stick it back on, but I can't mend the burst football, and Jack's going to be really upset about that. The Little Runt might send me mental, but he doesn't deserve to have his prize possessions trashed by tanked-up strangers.

I work my way through the house, just grateful that I haven't found any condoms down the back of the radiators or dangling from a plant, and drag the black bin bag outside into the garden and start poking about in the bushes with a pea stick.

The paracetamol and water combo has finally kicked in, and the sunnies help with the light, but I still have to move *really* slowly otherwise I get a violent attack of the dizzies.

The garden seems to have come off better than the house. It's mostly fag ends and crushed cans on the lawn. I've heard about teenage parties where the entire living room has been taken out and rearranged in the garden, and the garden has been dug up and put in the living room, so it could be worse.

And then I see it.

The door to Google's hutch is open and the wire run attached to his cage has been moved. There's no sign of the guinea pig, but instead, my teddy and Jack's toy Dalek are doing rude things.

I start hunting around, poking in the foliage with the stick. Google can't have got far. He's fat and old and our garden has a fence round it . . . other than the bit that's broken.

But Google is nowhere to be found.

The mental mammal has done a runner.

Chapter Sixteen

I thought about rescuing the rutting toys, putting the hutch back together and then waiting until dark when I could creep out, dig a hole under the run and make out that Google had tunnelled his way to freedom, but I can't face the thought of digging with a hangover, and as he's never shown any Houdini instincts in the past, I doubt anyone would believe me.

When I finally fessed up to Mum he'd gone AWOL she went nuclear, banned me from watching TV for a week, confiscated my moby and sent me to my room with an order that I write a list of *everything* that's been damaged as I'm going to have to pay for it all.

It's lucky I can use the thigh-crusher to tap out the list as I'm not sure I feel strong enough to hold a pen, so I'm sitting on the bed, propped up with pillows, tapping away, trying not to think about Claudia (and possibly Jags) rolling on my duvet.

So far the list includes, but is not limited to:

Repairing broken kitchen window.

New football for Jack.

Possibly new goalie for table football if glue surgery doesn't repair fatal neck injury.

Replacement cost of everything in the fridge and wine under the stairs.

New wine glasses.

Cleaning stuff, especially bleach, extra bin bags and carpet cleaner.

Two new airbeds to replace punctured ones.

Sanding marks out of kitchen table, or, if unable to be scrubbed out, a new table.

New sofa if smell of beer doesn't come out and throw doesn't cover burn marks.

New throw.

1 litre of magnolia paint to paint out red wine murder-like stains on hall wall.

New guinea pig if mental mammal doesn't waddle home.

Replacement of missing iPod which some lowlife must have swiped on the way out as revenge for being chucked out on to the street by Mum and Phil.

With not being able to text I'm going mad wondering what's happening with Lucy and Sorrel. I still don't know how Lucy and James got home, but I expect if they hadn't turned up we'd have heard by now. Bella will have given Lucy a lecture about lying, and Yolanda is probably deeply disappointed that Sorrel got trashed on ordinary vodka, rather than some stuff made from ethically farmed Fair Trade organic grain.

Nuclear Mental Mum sticks her head around the bedroom door. I've ditched the sunnies and now I can feel the full force of her anger rays boring into me like lasers.

'I've been next door and the Skinners say Google's not in their garden,' she snaps. 'He could be anywhere by now. How are you going to explain this to Jack?'

I hang my head extra low so my chin almost touches my chest, firstly to show that I'm sorry, but mostly to avoid catching sight of Mum's death-ray eyes. She's starting to look possessed, like something out of a horror movie, and I'm worried that as well as the possessed eyes her head is going to start spinning before it explodes.

I'm not sure how I'm going to explain to my little bro that his pet guinea pig has done a runner, or that his football is trashed, his duvet smells like a brewery, there's grass stains on his Dalek and his goalie is headless. I'm sort of hoping he won't notice, but in case he does, I tap out:

At least 24 tubs of Pot Noodles to say sorry to Jack for
breaking his possessions and losing the family pet.

'Well, you'd better think of something quickly as I'm off to pick him up from the Finkelsteins' now.'

Mum bangs the bedroom door unnecessarily hard and stomps down the stairs.

What do other people do when their pets go missing? I think to myself.

Celebrate that they don't have to clean poo and pee-soaked sawdust out once a week?

Buy a new one?

Think, I've done the whole guinea pig scene, let's move on to the real deal, a dog?

There's *no way* Mum will let me have a pupster now, not if I can't even look after a guinea pig. Dogs are *much* easier to lose. I'm always seeing posters with sad-looking mutts staring out, their distraught owners offering a reward for their safe return.

That's it!

A poster!

I'll type out a poster on the thigh-crusher and print it out. It won't be a very big poster because the printer only takes A4 paper, but it might help. The trouble is I've zero money for a reward; in fact, by the time I've paid for all the damage I'll have *minus* money, as I'll have to pledge all future Christmas and birthday cash to the Mortimer Road Party Disaster Relief Fund. Still, it's worth a try, and without my moby to text the girls and no iPod to listen to, I've got nothing else to do.

I open up a new Word document and start to create something. It's a bummer I haven't actually got round to sorting out the wireless Internet connection as I can't get on the Web in my room, which means I don't have a picture of a guinea pig to download. I decide to leave a space so that I can draw one in by hand. I fiddle about with the typeface and font, do some fancy lettering and a rather snazzy border, and print out ten copies.

The first few hand-drawn guinea pigs look more like giant mutant rats, but after a while they get better and less rat-like, and anyway, the big letters **MISSING GUINEA PIG** should give people a clue as to what the poster is about. I don't think he'll be far. He's probably just in someone's garden, gorging himself on grass and attacking anyone who dares come near him.

With the posters finished I need to get some drawing pins from the newsagent's so that I can stick them on trees and telegraph poles.

So as not to be out on the streets with even more mismatched boobs than I naturally possess, I remove the test chicken fillet which is all sweaty and seems to have given me a rash, grab my bag and head downstairs.

I've got my hand on the front door when a voice behind me says, 'Where do you think you're going?'

It's Phil. What with stressing over the AWOL mammal, my hangover and the Jags/Tits Out bedroom scenario I'd *completely* forgotten The Impostor might still be hanging around.

I swivel round, and instead of the kind, friendly face he usually wears Phil looks fed up and scarily angry. I can imagine him as a mean killing machine in the army, even if he says he was an engineer rather than a gun-toting shooter. Still, even if I've behaved badly and am *technically* in the wrong, it doesn't mean I owe it to Phil to be nice to him. It's Mum's house, not his, so she's the only one with the right to be mad at me.

'Just out.' I turn back to open the door.

'Oh, no you're not. You're staying here!'

I look over my shoulder, flashing him my best *Teenage in mega strop with mega hangover* glare, the first time I've tried this particular combo and one which I'm hoping will be devastatingly effective when coupled with a searingly sarcastic voice. 'I'm out to put up posters saying Google's missing.' I wave them at him.

'You're not going anywhere until your mum gets back.'

I shrug. I'm not taking orders from The Impostor. Anyway, I need to get the leaflets pinned up before someone runs over Google with a lawnmower.

I go to leave but quick as a flash Phil leans over me, slamming the door. I'm *that* close to losing a nail in the door and if I had done it would have been a *complete* disaster as it's taken me *weeks* to get them this long.

I freak.

'What the hell do you think you're doing?' I scream at him. I'd thought my headache was a bit better, but the screaming seems to have brought it back to life. 'I nearly lost a finger!' It was only ever going to be the tip of a nail, but a severed finger sounds more dramatic.

'I've told you, Electra!' Phil's voice is raised. 'You're not going anywhere!'

'Don't you *dare* tell me what to do!' I realize that without meaning to I've actually sort of spat at Phil as there's a frothy bit on the end of his nose. 'You're not my mum and you're *certainly* not my dad. I'll do what I want, when I want, *if* I want!'

By now Phil is blocking the front door, tattooed arms folded, face murderous, even with the blob of spit on his beak.

'That's just typical of you, Electra Brown,' he snaps back. 'I want! I want! I want! The chant of a selfish spoilt little brat! You were determined to wreck our night away, ruin things for your mum, and now you have done. Congratulations!'

'It's a pleasure!' I scream. Two can play the sarcasm game, and I like to think of myself as a bit of a sarcameister. 'Anytime!'

'Oh, grow up and start taking some responsibility for your actions!' Phil shouts. 'And until you do, get back to your room.'

I laugh in his face. Not a proper happy laugh, of course. A sarky *You can't say anything to hurt me because you're nothing!* type of laugh.

'Yeah. Right. Like I'm really going to take orders from a mobile grease monkey!'

I hadn't meant to say that, in fact, I hadn't even thought of the phrase since Dad said it in Pizza Hut. Still, I'm glad it slipped out because Phil looks *totally* shocked.

'A what . . . ?'

'Shall I repeat it slowly so you understand?' I say this in such a sneery way I know that Sorrel would be *mega* proud of me. 'A – Mobile – Grease – Monkey. A mechanic without a garage. An – Oily – Rag. I'm not surprised your wife ran off with her fitness instructor. You're such a sad loser!'

I take advantage of the fact that Phil is looking

shell-shocked that I've just totally dissed his career of choice, dragged his ex-wife into the argument and called him a saddo, and lunge towards the front door and yank it open. I'm about to bolt down the steps when I see Mum hurrying up them, Jack dawdling behind her. I *could* rush down, knock my mother out of the way and leapfrog over Jack, but I don't think that would help matters, so I stand in the doorway looking defiant, or at least I hope that's how I look. To be honest I'm starting to feel a bit shaky, and I don't think it's just the hangover.

'What on earth's going on?' Mum demands, pushing past me into the house. 'I could hear you shouting from the street.'

'He told me to go to my room!' I say.

Really annoyingly I start to cry. This was not in the *I'm a hard cow, see if I care* plan.

'She was trying to go out,' Phil explains. 'I told her to stay here until you got back.'

'I was going out to put up notices about Google!' I shriek, waving the posters so close to his face I can hear the paper scrape across his stubble. 'He's probably had his head chopped off by a lawnmower now and if he has, it's *all* your fault.'

I tear the posters up into little pieces and throw them in the air.

As bits of paper flutter to the carpet, Jack bursts into tears and starts screaming at Phil, 'Murderer! Murderer!'

I'm screaming at Phil. 'See what you've done!'

Mum is screaming at both of us to shut up.

And Phil?

Phil the hard man is crying.

Chapter Seventeen

'You slid *all* the way down Jags and you didn't feel a thing?' Sorrel asks as we sit in first reg on Monday morning waiting for Frosty the Penguin to waddle in.

'Not even a little thing?' Lucy giggles.

'Nothing,' I groan, resting my head on the desk in shame.

'No wonder I call him El Dwarfo,' says Sorrel. 'Small in every department.'

I can't even be bothered to glare at her for dissing The Spanish Lurve God. I haven't the energy. Everything has gone wrong. *Everything*.

As well as having a huge repair bill hanging over me, a chin full of throbbing spots and a little brother who keeps coming up to me and hissing, 'Murderer' in my ears once he realized I was part of Google's escape plan, I'm grounded. No one has said for how long, but

I'm guessing for the rest of my living-at-home life.

Of course, grounded only means you have to stay at home when you'd rather be out having fun. It doesn't mean you can't go to school, which just makes the whole grounding scene so inconsistent, especially as there's nothing to stop me bunking off school and spending the day enjoying myself, other than the threat of a letter home and more parental aggro.

And it's not just me that's in trouble.

Mum is too.

Lucy says Bella's going to ring Mum to discuss what happened. She's hopping mad, but not about the fact that Lucy lied, or that James was totally buzzed and fell over in the garden crushing most of Bella's rare black dahlias. No, Bella is annoyed that her children were thrown out of the house and left wandering the streets at one in the morning. But, as I explained to Luce, Mum couldn't run them home because Sorrel was in a voddy-induced coma on the back seat of the Focus and Phil was taking *her* home.

Yolanda was apparently pretty relaxed about her daughter being off her head as she thought it would put her off booze for life. Jasmine, however, wasn't as, like me, Sorrel was barfing into a bucket all night. Unlike me she was doing it from a top bunk, and her aim wasn't always that good. Apparently Jas freaked when she went to put on her trainers because she found Parsley the cat slurping vomit out of them.

Even though I could have done with a day in bed, I couldn't face staying at home with Nuclear Mad Mum, even if she'd let me. I thought about bunking off and spending the day wandering around the shops, but my legs still feel a bit wobbly, and with all my debts I can't afford to sit all day in Burger King or KFC, plus it's probably better that I try and keep myself occupied as all sorts of terrors keep fluttering through my butterfly brain.

As my hangover wore off, more party horrors came back to me such as some boys in the kitchen filling condoms with water until they burst. I didn't see any burst condoms when I was clearing up, so it either means I've missed them, or Mum found them. It's all too horrible to think about.

Then I remembered a group of the QB poshies trying on some of Mum's clothes, parading up and down the hall, cackling with catty snobby laughter over the elasticated waists and huge T-shirts. At one point I saw a girl wearing one of Mum's bras on her head, shrieking over the fact that her head easily fitted into one of the greying lace cups, whilst some cow with a face like a horse and a voice like a donkey was braying, 'Oh, God.

The sad cow must be either a porker or a porno with front bumps that huge!'

I should have wrapped Mum's bap-pack round the girl's neck and pulled it until she sank to the floor gasping for air, but I didn't. I just left them to it.

I don't know why I didn't do anything to stop them. When they were trashing Mum's wardrobe it wasn't that I was drunk, it's just that I felt *totally* out of my depth and *completely* overwhelmed by what was going on. Like a rabbit caught in car headlights, instead of doing *something* I did *nothing* because I was paralysed with fear. And *then* I became paralysed with drink. And I don't really know why I drank so much. I didn't enjoy it, and I don't even like it, but I didn't know what else to do. Everyone else seemed to be doing *something*, snogging or dancing or wrecking the house whilst I was just pushing past people I'd never met, going from room to room feeling more and more panicky.

And then there was the Jags episode.

I've been over it time and time again in my mind. I've spent hours making myself look good for him and learning things to impress him. I've wasted days hanging around the sports centre with my badminton racket trying to look sporty. Weeks wandering round and round Eastwood Circle trying to look glamorous in case he just popped out of HMV or was browsing in JD Sports. Years daydreaming about our non-existent life together. And I blew any chance I might have had by collapsing in a dribbling heap at his feet, having told him the only snogging I do is on my arm. Is it any wonder he didn't show me then and there just how high on the S-Scale he could be?

One thing's for certain. I am never *ever* going to drink to excess again.

'Great party!'

I look up to see Claudia Barnes has come into class with Nat and Tam.

I'm mega-furious with all of them. I know that I lied to Mum, but when I was formulating my non-party-sleepover plan I didn't reckon on the tarty trio issuing an open-house invitation to anyone they could think of. Still, I'm relieved to see that Tits Out isn't wearing Jags's tie, though she does have a ring of hickeys around her neck, presumably a souvenir from her encounter with either Buzzer or Jags or both.

I rummage around in my bag until I find what I'm looking for.

'I found this under my bed. It's yours I presume?'

It's the chicken fillet. I was going to brandish it on the bus in the hope of humiliating her, but Mum ran me to school to make sure I got there, and anyway, it's better if the whole class can see Claudia Barnes wither and die from fake boob embarrassment.

I throw it across the classroom and it lands on the desk in front of her. As well as hair and bedroom dust, it's now got a layer of bag debris stuck to it. It looks really gross, like a chicken breast dusted in disgusting breadcrumbs. I'm pretty impressed that for someone who's crap at games I was such a good shot. It wouldn't have had the same effect if it had landed on Spud's head, or by The Penguin's swollen trotters.

Cool as a cucumber, Tits Out picks up the fillet, blows the stuff off it and purrs, 'Oh, thanks. I wondered where that had got to,' before tucking it into her bra in front of *everyone*.

I'm completely gobsmacked. I don't believe for one minute she's come to school lopsided. She's probably got a whole drawer of them in different sizes. But what sort of a girl is proud of the fact that one of her fake baps has been found under my bed? A super slag! Tits Out really is Queen of the Sleazers.

Tammy Two-Names leans over to me. 'God, your old man went mental when he broke up the party,' she sneers, her braces glinting under the fluorescent strip lights. 'He *so* doesn't know how to have a good time, does he?'

I give her what I just know is a first-class withering stare, and say, 'Oh get lost, metal mouth.'

We're moving between maths and physics when I bump into Freak Boy. Literally. He's scrabbling on the floor picking up books and papers he's dropped. Ahead of him Pinhead and Spud stand jeering.

'Sorry,' he mutters, as people stamp on his stuff as they go past.

'S'OK,' I say as Luce bends down to help him.

'Did they push you?' I ask him.

He doesn't reply, but the back of his neck goes crimson, so the answer is probably *Yes*.

I feel a bit of a bitch just standing around, so I pick up the odd sheet of paper, just to show willing. Sorrel obviously doesn't feel any sympathy as she just stands leaning against the wall, watching us, chewing bubble gum.

'I hear you had a good party,' FB says. 'Well, wild anyway.'

He must have heard someone mention it when he was lurking. No one would have told him. I sort of want to say that if I'd been going to have a proper party I would have invited him, but of course even if I was, I wouldn't, so I don't.

'It all got out of hand,' I say. 'The house was wrecked, our guinea pig got let out and is still missing, and my little bro's heartbroken.'

'I believe guinea pigs first came from South America,' Freak Boy says.

'Well, Google's from 14 Mortimer Road,' I say, realizing with horror that I've told FB my address.

'I think that's it,' Lucy says, handing him the last pile of books covered with footprints. 'And in future, just keep away from Pinhead and his mates.'

'They're tossers,' I add, still not having forgiven them for ignoring me.

'Nah, you don't want to avoid them,' says Sorrel, blowing a huge bubble which bursts. She gathers up the pink goo with her tongue and starts chewing again. 'You want to beat them to a pulp.'

Chapter Eighteen

It's been hell at Mortimer Road since the party.

The Impostor has been round every night since Sunday, so although they haven't actually told me that I can't come downstairs, I don't want to be around The Love Birds unless it's an absolute emergency like I have to go to the fridge, but it means this has been the fourth night in a row I've been stuck upstairs in my room, lying on my bed, staring into space with not even any decent music to listen to because of the lowlife iPod-swiper.

There's been no Dad contact since the night of Operation Bald Eagle, but I've considered phoning him to confront him over lying about Candy and Caroline, and whilst I'm giving him the full-on guilt vibes, remind him that he and Nana still owe me a birthday present, and please could I have a new iPod, preferably a pink Nano?

But so far I haven't because there are several flaws with this idea.

One, as my moby has been confiscated as part of my punishment I'd have to use the house phone which means going downstairs.

Two, if I email him then that's another trip down to the land of the smoochy ones.

And three, if I did get in touch, I'd have to come up with some story about how I lost the old one, like it was stolen by a gang of hooligans on the bus, as I'm not sure that fessing up that it was nicked during a teenage party whilst Mum was away with Phil would go down well. I also have the sort of feeling that Mum wouldn't want Dad to know what had happened, though as Dad has one of his access days to Jack soon I guess The Little Runt will give him all the gory details.

I had hoped that by the time I came home from school on Monday Mum might be a bit calmer, but a series of unfortunate events caused her to crank the anger-meter to a new level.

Event number one was that when she went to get some pizzas out of the freezer she found someone had puked in it, and there was frozen vomit over everything, so she ordered me to chip the iced barf out, bit by vomity bit.

Secondly, as I was forcing some pizza down, trying to

forget that it had been coated in vomit, Jack pointed at the ceiling and shouted, 'You had balloons at your party!'

It wasn't a balloon. It was a condom dangling over the kitchen light.

Mum glared at me so I stood on a chair and poked at it with a broom handle to get it down, but unfortunately it still had quite a bit of water in it, so as it fell to earth it showered Mum and Jack with liquid. Jack wanted to blow it up and put some string round it, but not surprisingly Mum wouldn't let him, so he had a really stompy-feet-type tantrum.

Then Bella Malone phoned and lectured Mum for over an hour. I didn't hear it of course, as by that time I'd escaped to my room, but at school on Tuesday Luce told me that she'd hung over the stairs at her house and heard The Neat Freak banging on about responsibilities, how it was understandable I'd gone off the rails now I was from a broken home, and had we considered family counselling?

So all in all, it's probably safer to stay stuck up here with only the radio and its cheesy tunes for company.

I hear the doorbell go.

'Electra!' Phil shouts up the stairs.

I'm in no hurry to go down. Unlike Mum, Phil's been trying to be normal to me over the last few days, but I'm still giving him the full *Winter in Siberia* treatment for calling me a selfish spoilt brat.

'Electra! You've got a visitor!'

If I don't go down he'll come up and invade my space.

I drag myself off the bed. It's probably Bella Malone. Lucy said her mum was threatening to come round to try to organize a family conference.

I arrange my face into its most sullen *What?* type look, and amble downstairs.

It's not Bella Malone.

It's the complete opposite of Mrs Perfect.

Standing in our hall, looking down at his feet, holding out a pale-blue box with TIFFANY & CO stamped across the top in classy black capital letters, is Freak Boy.

This is terrible! What do I do? Here is the school's most unfortunate boy, in my house, about to give me a present from Tiffany! If I'm not to encourage him I should really tell him to get lost and take the beautiful box with him.

But a bauble from Tiffany?

No way!

Perhaps I'll take it and pretend someone else gave it to me. But what if there's a price to pay for taking the bling box, like going on a date with him? There's a name for women who go out with people they can't stand just to get money and presents. Gold-diggers and prostitutes.

Can I sink so low as to accept a gift knowing there are probably strings attached?

I take the box.

It's really heavy and must contain some *seriously* expensive bling. It's obviously either a late birthday gift, or a trinket to thank me for helping him when he hurt his ankle or . . .

'I'm sorry. I think I've found your guinea pig dead at the bottom of our garden.'

I almost drop the box with shock. It doesn't hold some expensive present. It's got a corpse in it! Perhaps I can tip out the dead mammal and keep the box? I scrabble at the lid.

'I've sealed it so no one can look in,' explains Freak Boy. 'It's only a bit of him as I think a fox must have got to him first, but if your pet had toffee-coloured fur, it's probably him.'

I don't know what to say. It's not every day you get a gift-boxed stiff.

'I've wrapped him in a freezer bag,' FB says. 'It's not surprising he got eaten. Did you know there are roughly a quarter of a million foxes in Britain?'

Phil had made himself scarce, but now comes into the hall.

'Ooh, a present,' he says. 'How lovely. Anything nice?'

As it's hot and no one wants a rotting guinea pig sitting in the fridge alongside the salad, we decide to hold the funeral immediately. Phil asked Freak Boy if he wanted to stay, but much to my relief he didn't. He scurried off, completely oblivious to the fact that most girls don't want a fox-munched mammal as a present, even if it is beautifully wrapped.

Whilst Phil dug a grave at the bottom of the garden alongside the one for Pippin the hamster and various unnamed goldfish, Mum told Jack that Google had gone to guinea pig heaven, which she said was just like our back garden, but with a lawn filled with extra juicy dandelion leaves and no hungry foxes.

It's Jack's first proper experience of death as he wasn't born when Granddad Kevin drowned in the concrete pit, and Pippin and the fish died before he was old enough to know what was going on. He does now, and he looks heartbroken as we stand around the deep hole peering down at the Tiffany box.

I'm heartbroken too. It seems such a terrible waste. Not of a guinea pig life, but of a seriously gorgeous box.

Jack had wanted to look in and check that it really was Google and that I wasn't just playing some sort of sick joke to upset him. I thought he'd be more upset to see only half of his beloved pet, so I lied and told him I'd checked and it *was* Google, but that once the box-coffin lid was closed and sealed it was unlucky to open it again, and if we did it would mean that Arsenal would *definitely* be relegated next season and Google wouldn't want that, would he?

Jack stands by the graveside clutching a small cross Phil helped him make out of lolly sticks. He's tried to write Google's name on it in marker pen but ran out of space, so it just says *Goog*.

'Do you want to say something?' Mum gently asks Jack who's sobbing snotty graveside sobs.

'Like what?' Jack replies.

'Well, people sometimes have their favourite songs played at funerals,' Phil says. 'Something that meant something special to them.'

Jack thinks for a moment, nods and starts singing.

'Good old Arsenal, we're proud to say that name.

And while we sing this song we'll win the game!'

I'm sure it's not what any of us had in mind, but the sight of my little brother sobbing his song out, whilst holding his lolly-stick cross, really gets to me.

Phil puts an arm around his bony little shoulders. Mum starts crying, and Phil puts his other arm round her.

No one comforts me.

Perhaps they realized I was more upset about the box than the bit-of-the-pet-in-the-box. But, looking at the sad faces around me, I realize this is *all* my fault! I can blame the tarty trio for inviting their friends, and their friends for being teenage terrorists and trashing the house and opening Google's hutch. I can point the finger at the others who brought alcohol when I'd intended to stuff my face with Twiglets and pizzas rather than Bacardi Breezers. But the fact of the matter is, the start of this chain of events began with a lie. My lie. I went behind Mum's back when she trusted me. And now Google is dead, wrapped in a freezer bag and sealed in a Tiffany box at the bottom of a trench.

As Phil begins to fill in the hole, my chest feels as if it's being crushed. There's a lump in my throat and my eyes are blinded with tears as Jack puts the lolly-stick cross on the mound of earth and blows a kiss towards the grave.

I'm surprised to be so upset. I hated Google when he was alive. It was Jack who wanted a guinea pig. Jack who named the tiny toffee-coloured lump Google because he thought it was the funniest name he'd ever heard of. I didn't like Google from the start. I wanted a pupster to cuddle and take out for walks when I might bump into Jags, and I'd look a right prat walking down the road with a guinea pig on a lead. But then maybe I wasn't that nice to Google. When I fed him I used to fend him off wearing an oven glove and holding a badminton racket. Perhaps he knew I thought he was a poor substitute for a dog.

But he was part of our family and he made Jack happy. He didn't deserve to die.

Sometimes you don't realize what you've had until it's far too late.

Chapter Nineteen

This last week has taught me some valuable lessons:

Don't lie unless it's for a good reason as it can lead to all sorts of grief, not to mention mammal murder.

Don't get so drunk that you completely humiliate yourself in front of a Lurve God, and can't remember whether it was his jeans or his boxer shorts you've peeled off his luscious bod.

Don't count your Tiffany boxes until they're opened.

Don't let people you don't know into your house to try on your mum's mega bras.

Do remember that you've only got one family and, whatever you do, however badly you behave, however many lies you've told and however annoyed with you they get, the chances are they still love you.

Which means I still want to see Dad.

I think it was Google's funeral that did it. Dad wouldn't

win any prizes for being the world's number one dad, but he's the only one I've got, so as Jack put the lolly-stick cross on the little mound of earth and I was sobbing and feeling sorry for myself, I decided I'd better make the most of Dad while I can. If I don't, I can see us drifting apart.

At the heart of all the recent problems has been that I've been upset about Dad going off with Candy, and Mum getting close to Phil. I hate to admit it, but both Mum and Phil are right. You can't turn back the clock, and it's about time I grew up and got used to the fact that Mum and Dad are getting divorced and that they have new lives. I even apologized to Phil for being a bitch to him, not face to face of course, but a note saying, *Soz I was so rude to you. It woz the drink. Electra x* which I left under the windscreen wiper of his AA van. I didn't mean to put the kiss at the end, but when I did I thought I might as well leave it there.

Anyway, I decided I really wanted to see Dad, so I rang him during first break on Thursday morning, and said could I come round for tea on Friday night about six-thirty-ish? I think he was pretty surprised to hear my voice because as my moby is still quarantined as part of the grounding I'd used Lucy's phone, but especially because I've never wanted to go to the flat, not when Candy was living there anyway. But now she's gone and he's living on his own, it seems like a good idea.

When I asked Mum if I could go round she seemed a bit surprised too. Now that the stain on the wall has been painted out, the carpet's been cleaned and there's no vomit in the freezer, she's begun to thaw out a bit. Although a few days ago I was grounded she's now given me back my moby, and even offered to run me over as long as Dad brings me home. I expect she has other motives than to get father and daughter bonding. She probably wants some serious sofa-time with Phil.

So now I'm sitting in the car on the way to Dad's, starving, and wondering whether he'll cook or we'll get a take out.

'What number did you say it was?' Mum asks as we crawl along Aldbourne Road.

'22,' I say, though the big blue and white van with a huge plunger down the side gives the address away.

We pull up, I clamber out and ring the bell marked *Brown*, and as I hear someone coming down the stairs I turn to Mum, wave, and she zooms off.

When the door opens Dad looks slightly surprised to see me.

'Oh! Hi, Electra!'

He hugs me. He's *definitely* getting fatter. His moobs feel huge!

'You did remember I was coming round?' I ask, following him up the stairs.

'Of course!' Dad replies, not entirely convincingly. 'Come on in. I've just got to make a quick phone call.'

Whilst Dad goes into another room with his moby I look around.

I've never really given much thought to Dad's flat, but I guess I always assumed it would be a bit sad and bare. If I thought about it at all I imagined him slumped on a black leather sofa with a can of beer, watching football on a widescreen plasma TV surrounded by bare walls, and shelves empty but for a few dodgy DVDs stacked on them.

I'd forgotten that Candy had a hand in the decorating. And Candy Baxter wasn't just The Bitch Troll. She was obviously Queen of the Tassels.

Flat A, 22 Aldbourne Road is like living in the soft-furnishings department of John Lewis. The dark-red sofa is outlined with red piping and is piled high with cushions, most with tassels, some with fringes. A line of tassels runs across the window which is framed by heavy cream curtains held back by huge tennis-ball-sized red and gold tassels. There's fringing on the rugs, bows on the chairs around the glass dining table which has a pair of crystal candlesticks on it and, instead of the bare walls I'd imagined, it looks as if Candy took her decorating inspiration from a curry house, there's so much gold and cream flocked wallpaper.

All I can say to Dad is, 'It's not like Mortimer Road, is it?' and he laughs, especially when I go to take an apple from the fruit bowl on the table and find it's plastic.

It's good here with Dad. Relaxed. *So* much better than sitting in a restaurant trying to make conversation. Going out with Dad was always a bit of a strain, trying to think of places to go, things to say, always being surrounded by other people, but this feels normal. Well, as normal as being with your father in a strange tassel-festooned flat can be.

I've made Dad a cup of tea in the kitchen which has grapes stencilled around the door and a collection of frog fridge magnets, and we're both just slumped on the sofa whilst I flick through the channels to try and find something we can both watch.

'Shall we ring for a pizza?' I say. 'But nothing with pepperoni.'

'Good idea,' Dad replies, and starts shuffling a pile of papers on the glass coffee table.

He's still hunting for the pizza delivery leaflet when a buzzer goes.

He gets up and leans into the intercom thing on the wall. 'Hello?'

'It's me, sugar plum!' a woman's shrill voice says. 'And I've got dinner!'

Dad looks embarrassed. 'It's Caroline!' he croaks, pressing a button.

He opens the door and I hear the clickity-click-clack of high heels coming up the stairs, and the smell of curry followed by a bony woman with reddish-blonde poker-straight shoulder-length hair, orange fake-tan skin, wearing a tight black trouser suit over a little white top. She's carrying what looks like a very expensive black footballers'-wives-style handbag in one hand, and a brown carrier bag with grease creeping up the side in the other.

'The Rose Tandoori's Special Set Balti Dinner for two!' she announces.

And then she sees me. She doesn't smile or say hello, she just stands frozen on the cream shagpile.

'Caroline, this is my daughter, Electra. Electra, this is Caroline,' Dad calls out over his shoulder as he takes the carrier bag into the kitchen.

It's Dad's divorce lawyer. Caroline Cole. The woman Candy told me about.

Caroline thaws her face just enough to manage a grin

214

so painfully forced it looks as if someone is dragging either side of her mouth open with a couple of fish hooks.

'Hello!' Her voice sounds friendly but her eyes are dead. 'I've been looking forward to meeting you. I've heard so much about you.'

She dumps her bag on to the sofa beside me (it's a Chloé – she must be minted!) and follows Dad into the kitchen.

I shuffle to the other end of the sofa, turn the telly down and listen.

'I forgot she was coming.' Dad's whispering. 'When she turned up, I left you a message on your mobile.'

'I let my battery run down,' Caroline says. 'I didn't get the message.'

I get up and go into the kitchen. Caroline is leaning against the kitchen units, arms folded, dragging on a cigarette. With her glassy eyes, bony frame, orange skin, and lips pouting around the cancer stick, she reminds me of a kipper. A kipper in designer clothes.

'Look, would you rather I went?' I ask. The bonding evening is ruined for me. There's something deeply dodgy about this woman, though I don't know what.

'Not at all. We'll find a way of sharing two vegetable samosas between three, won't we, Rob?' The Kipper says brightly. 'It'll be lovely to spend some time with you.'

I'm sure I can feel an icy draft as she heads back to the living room.

Dad and I divide the meal between three plates, and then Dad takes his and hers and sits beside her on the sofa, and I'm left looking around for somewhere to perch. In the end I sit at the dining table behind the sofa with my plate and a pile of poppadoms, staring at the backs of their heads above the red fringing, wondering whether I could lob a chunk of chicken tikka into The Kipper's designer handbag without either of them noticing. I probably could. They seem much more interested in a programme on mating seagulls than they are in talking to me.

One of the seagulls is sitting on a nest looking a bit sulky, probably because there are four eggs under her and she can't move.

Dad's moby goes.

There's lots of muttering and under-breath swearing and then he's up and grabbing his van keys.

'Sorry, girls. Got to go back to the warehouse. That was the alarm company. Apparently the damn thing's going off. It's probably that new cleaner we've got. Next time it goes off, I'll dock her wages.'

'Oh, sweet pea!' The Kipper whines. 'Can't somebody else do it?'

Dad jangles his keys impatiently. "Fraid not. I'm the main key-holder. Won't be long. Have fun, you two!'

And then he's gone. Out of the flat, down the stairs and away in his van.

It's just me, The Kipper, a curry and the seagull whose eggs have now hatched.

'Oh, the poor thing!' I gasp, looking away from the TV as one of the baby birds falls out of the nest and tumbles down the cliff face, bouncing off rocks before plopping into the crashing waves below. After Google's murder I still feel a bit sensitive to violent deaths, even if they are by natural causes.

'Survival of the fittest,' says The Kipper, lighting up a cigarette. 'You should remember Darwin's theory, Electron.'

Her tone has changed from friendly to frosty.

I knew it! The woman is a complete phoney! She was all *How lovely to meet you!* rubbish, and now Dad's gone she's turned into The Kipper from hell. I bet even her designer handbag is a fake.

She waves a bony orange hand in the air. 'Pass me a poppadom, Electron.'

'It's Electra,' I say, spitting on one and rubbing the spit in with my finger before passing it to her. 'Stop calling me Electron.'

'Well, if the name fits,' she says.

She bites into the gobbed poppadom and I snigger under my breath.

I avoid a viciously spicy and almost certainly diarrhoea-inducing lamb bhuna, push some cold pilau rice around my plate and wonder what to do next.

And then the seagull programme finishes. The Kipper switches off the TV, lights up another cigarette, blows a few smoke rings in the air, picks up a magazine and *totally* ignores me.

The atmosphere is so cold it's like sitting in a tasselled igloo.

'You don't like me very much, do you?' I say, trying to break the ice after what seems like *hours*.

Silence.

'Why?'

Icy Silence.

I get up and stand in front of her. She keeps puffing and flicking, *completely* blanking me.

'Hey! I asked you a question.'

Finally she raises her fish-head and looks at me with dead eyes.

'Listen up, kid,' she drawls. 'Around your dad I'll be nice to you. In fact, so he thinks I'm a wonderful person, I'll be *very* nice to you. But the *moment* he's not looking,

218

as far as I'm concerned, you'll go back to being an inconvenient and rather nasty reminder of his past life.'

She looks back down at her mag and I have an almost overwhelming urge to beat her around the head with her posh handbag.

'I'll tell him you're a devious two-faced fish and that you've been nasty to me and then let's see who he'll believe!' I snap back. 'Blood is thicker than water, remember?'

The Kipper snorts. 'In that case I'll just deny everything and say it's another one of your silly little teenage plans to try and get your parents back together.' She gives a smug smile. 'It wouldn't be the first time you've lied, would it? And remember, I'm a lawyer, which means I'm so good at lying, I get paid for doing it!'

Dad has obviously told her about Operation Bald Eagle. Once he sees Jack this weekend and he finds out about Google and the party I'm going to be exposed as a multiple fibber.

I grab my bag and stomp off to the loo, not because I need to pee, but because I have to get away from The Evil Kipper if I'm not to grab the lit fag from her pouting gob and stuff it up her nose.

I sit on the closed loo seat with its pink shaggy cover and mentally add Candy to the list of people and pets I didn't appreciate at the time. I wish she was here now. I hated her gushing about how we could be friends and suggesting we went out for meals, but at least she wasn't a kippered fake.

I ring Sorrel and flush the loo just as she answers in case The Kipper is listening at the door, gathering more evidence against me.

'What exactly is an electron?' I whisper down the phone, very fast, so as to get my question in quickly.

Yolanda only lets Sorrel use her moby for three minutes at a time because she's convinced that young brain cells become fried by microwaves if they're clamped to your head for any longer. It's a pain, but the trade off for the three-minute warning is that Yolanda pays Sorrel's moby bill.

'Where are you?' Sorrel asks. 'What's that gurgling in the background?'

'I'm sitting on the loo at Dad's.'

Sorrel makes gagging sounds and I have to reassure her that I'm not actually peeing and speaking at the same time, and yes, I will wash my hands afterwards, but please can she hurry up and tell me what an electron is before the three minutes is up as Dad's new tart keeps calling me one.

There's a brief silence and then Sorrel says, 'The total cow!'

'Why? What is it?'

'It's a particle that exerts a negative charge on its surroundings and can cause interference. Or something like that.'

'You are *such* a closet egg-head,' I say, furious at The Kipper, but totally impressed that Sorrel knew. 'You'd make a great geek.'

'Nah,' she laughs. 'I was on the computer downloading some tunes when you rang, and I just did a quick search.'

I didn't tell The Kipper I was going.

I hid in the bathroom for a while just to keep out of her way. I looked in the cabinet for girly signs such as Tampax and perfumed deodorant, but there was only shaving foam, plasters and ancient razors crusted with dried whiskers. Either The Kipper brings her own stuff, or she's not yet at the relationship stage of keeping sanitary supplies at Dad's. There might still be time to get rid of her before she gets her scaly orange tail firmly under the glass table.

I then sat on the side of the pink bath and fantasized about finding some nail scissors and marching out to cut off all the dangly bits on her designer bag, but as she's a lawyer and might sue me, I decided it wasn't worth it.

And then, when there was nothing else to look at and

no more bag vandalism to dream of, I just walked out, banging the front door as I went, and now I'm sitting in the fading light, on a wall, near the flat, kicking my heels against the brickwork, waiting for Dad to come home.

The *moment* he pulls up I'm going to tell him how mean The Kipper has been to me, maybe trying a few tears for maximum impact. Surely he won't keep seeing her then? I mean, I know he's never going to get back together with Mum, but he can't, he just absolutely can't carry on seeing that evil fish.

I look at my watch. Dad should be back soon. Time to prepare a distraught daughter face.

I squeeze out a few tears by remembering Jack singing at Google's funeral, but really they're half-hearted feeling-sorry-for-myself type of tears, so I rub my eyes until they water and my mascara runs.

But what about if he's not sure whether it's me or The Kipper who's telling the truth? What if he believes her rather than me? She's a trained lawyer and I'm just a fourteen-year-old schoolgirl. We're both good liars, but the difference is, she's a professional and I'm still an amateur.

I try and think what a proper lawyer would say. I sometimes come downstairs when Mum's watching some cheesy detective programme and they're always banging on about *gathering the evidence*.

That's what I need! Some hard evidence to get The Kipper into trouble.

I flirt with the idea of going back in and using my moby to record her saying vile things to me, but I'd have to ring the bell, and the thought of seeing her again is too horrible to contemplate.

I could report her for having an affair with one of her clients as surely that can't be allowed, but as fantastic as it would be if she got into serious trouble and lost her job, she might still see Dad.

Then I have the brilliant idea of slapping myself in the face and pretending that The Kipper did it. It's Friday, so any red marks will have faded by the time I get to school on Monday, and a couple of stinging red blotches across my face will really look convincing. If she can lie to Dad, so can I, and I know I said I wasn't going to lie unless it was for a good reason, but this is a *very* good reason.

I'm just slapping myself about my chops, trying to work up to a couple of really big stinging slaps, when a silver Mercedes estate pulls up beside me and the passenger door flies open.

'Electra?'

Bella Malone is bearing down on me like a blonde-bobbed rocket in the half-light. I can see Tom Malone in the driver's seat.

'Whatever is going on? Are you all right?' Bella asks.

I shrug. 'Not really,' I say, which is true, as I hadn't reckoned on my own strength and I've just *really* hurt my left cheek and my eyes are watering.

'I can't have you sitting on a wall on your own on a Friday night harming yourself,' Bella says. 'Shall we take you home?'

And then it hits me.

Dad will soon be back in the flat, sitting on the tasselled sofa with The Kipper. Mum will be at home snuggled on the beer-stained sofa with The Impostor. It's all very well trying to be grown up about everything, but at the end of the day they're both getting on with their lives whilst I'm not on anyone's sofa. I'm sitting on a brick wall, on a Friday night, on my own, biffing myself about the chops. How tragic is that?

'I've got nowhere to go,' I sob. 'I don't want to go home.'

Bella Malone grabs my hand and pulls me off the wall. 'Then come and spend some time with us.'

Chapter Twenty

I'm up in my room, pushing things into a bag to take to Lucy's house, crying. Proper crying, not crying-for-effect-type crying.

When we got back to Mortimer Road Bella marched into our house and took over, firing off instructions whilst Mum just stood there letting The Neat Freak organize my life.

'And bring your uniform too, Electra. Then you can go straight to school from our house on Monday morning,' Bella had said. 'I think you could all do with a break, don't you, Ellie? I'll keep an eye on her, especially after the problems of last weekend. She'll be safe with us.'

Given that I was standing in the hall probably looking trashed from hitting myself and sobbing, I thought Mum might have put up a bit more of a fight to keep her daughter from being a weekend foster kid with The Neat

Freak, but all she said was, 'Well, if you're sure.' She didn't even ask what went on at Dad's to get me into such a state.

Obviously neither Mum nor Dad want me around in case I disrupt their love lives. I've turned into a suitcase kid. Well, more of a Nike backpack and Top Shop handbag teenager actually.

Dad phoned as I was sitting in the back of Tom Malone's car. When he got back The Kipper told him the curry had given me an upset tummy and I'd wanted to go straight home. What really bugged me wasn't so much that she'd lied, but that Dad wasn't more suspicious of her story. She'd told him I'd said it was probably the aubergine bhaji that had made me rush to the loo, but he knows I wouldn't go anywhere near a chunk of the evil purple blob, so why didn't he think her tale of aubergine-induced trots a bit odd? He's obviously so in lust with her she could convince him black is white.

As I come back downstairs from my room the sound of low talking stops. They've obviously been yakking about me. I notice Bella glance past Mum into the front room. As I had to tidy it up after the party it's actually looking neater than it's been for ages, but I can see a flash of disgust cross Bella's face.

'Would you like me to recommend a cleaner, Ellie?'

she asks Mum. 'Someone who can help you get on top of things.'

Before Mum can answer Tom booms, 'Any more thoughts of putting this place on the market?'

I hold my breath, but luckily Mum shakes her head. She was going to sell the house soon after Dad moved out, but she's not mentioned anything recently so I haven't yet had to formulate a cunning plan to put potential buyers off. Telling them that the Skinners next door look like nice little old dears who wouldn't hurt a fly, but that really they run a twenty-four-hour crack den should do it.

'Are you sure you won't stay for a coffee?' Mum asks.

'No caffeine after eight o'clock for us, Ellie!' Bella says briskly. 'It's a stimulant and stimulants interfere with sleep.'

She picks up my bags. 'Let's go, Electra!' she says. 'Lucy will be thrilled to see you.'

'What are you doing here?' Lucy runs down the stairs and gives me a big hug. She's wrapped up in a yellow towelling dressing gown and smells all clean and fresh. I stink of curry and The Kipper's fag smoke.

'Electra is going to stay here for a while, just until things calm down at home,' Bella says.

A while? Just how long is a while? I thought I'd only agreed to a Friday night to Monday morning type of teenage fostering. Has Bella kidnapped me or was all that whispering in the hall Mum trying to get The Neat Freak to take me in on a more permanent basis?

'Electra can stay in your room, Lucy. I'll bring up some bedding.'

Lucy pulls an odd face. I've known her since we were four years old and this is an expression I don't recognize. Actually, that's not true. I have seen it before when we were about seven. We got left in a lift in a department store only because we were so busy playing with our Barbies we didn't follow Mum out. As the doors closed, Luce looked as if she wanted to scream but daren't, even though I was yelling my lungs out. It's the same *Help! I'm trapped!* look. For some reason, my best friend doesn't want me in her room.

Bella turns to her husband. 'Tom. Go into Lucy's room and pull out the spare bed, and put it so that the bedside table is between them. Make sure there's no dust on the frame and if you put it away after Electra leaves, turn the mattress.'

Lucy and I exchange glances.

I have a feeling this is going to be a long, tidy weekend.

* * *

If Luce was worried that she wouldn't get her beauty sleep because I'd spend all night rabbiting on about The Kipper, she needn't have done. I did intend to give her a detailed run-down of the evening but, after a shower which Bella insisted on, a peanut butter sandwich and a cup of hot milk, I climbed back into my T-shirt and knickers (I'd forgotten my nightie) and was asleep the moment my head hit the white 400 thread-count linen sheets that Bella had put on the pull-out bed next to Lucy's.

By the time I wake up, the sun is streaming through the cream blind, Lucy's bed is empty, the duvet fluffed up and the pillows straight.

It's nine o'clock.

I get up and pad towards the bathroom which is all sandy-coloured stone tiles, a gleaming white suite and a single cream orchid which I have to feel to see whether it's real or not. I'm glad it's fake as the curry last night has given me rampant gas. Bella might be so perfect she farts perfume, but I don't, and a real orchid might wilt in the toxic wind.

The shower last night means I can get away with just washing my face. I'll deal with the hair-washing issue later. I couldn't be bothered last night and I feel the same way this morning.

I'm about to run the taps when I realize that I've left my bath hat at home and Bella seems to have moved the one I used last night, probably to disinfect it. I don't want to get my fringe wet, so I take off yesterday's knickers and put them on my head as an emergency hairband.

'Electra! Are you up?' Bella Malone's crisp tones are floating up the stairs as I'm splashing water on my face. 'Cereal or scrambled eggs?'

I come out of the bathroom with a wet face, my Friday knickers on my head, wearing a T-shirt.

'Cereal's fine for me, thanks!' I shout down, dabbing my face with a towel.

And then I see them.

Standing in the hall, looking up the stairs at me, their golf clubs leaning by the front door.

Tom Malone, James Malone and Jags.

I want to die.

I want to spontaneously combust even if it does mean leaving a pile of grey ash on Bella's polished dark-wood floor.

I'm standing on a Saturday morning with a pair of knickers saying *Friday* on my head, but no knickers at all covering what Grandma Stafford always primly calls my *front bottom*, and not only that, I'm standing so that The Spanish Lurve God can look straight up at me. Even if he

230

didn't want to, he's *forced* into eyeballing my privates!

I shriek, pull the front of my T-shirt down, run back to Lucy's room, and wonder if it really is possible to die of shame.

I'm sitting on the edge of the bed hyperventilating with shock when Lucy comes in. I can tell from the look on her face that my gynaecological bits have been the topic of conversation downstairs.

'They saw me,' I wail. 'They saw bits only a doctor should see.'

Lucy is in hysterics. 'No, they didn't see anything at the front, but apparently they got a great view of your butt when you pulled the front of your T-shirt down and ran off.'

'Electra, can I have a word?' Bella Malone asks as I'm forcing myself to swallow the breakfast cereal which is rabbit food rather than Shreddies.

She turns to Lucy. 'Just because Electra is staying doesn't mean that we can't stick to the timetable.' She glances up at what looks like a giant laminated spreadsheet pinned to the kitchen wall. 'This morning I want you to concentrate on phrases you might need if you become ill in France.'

The way Bella says this isn't so much a suggestion as an

order, and Lucy trots off like a well-behaved dog.

'Now, about the bathroom . . .'

'I'm *so* sorry about that,' I say. 'It's just I forgot my bath hat and my nightie and then I didn't realize there were others at the bottom of the stairs and . . .'

Bella raises her hand to silence me. 'It wasn't specifically about that, though I do hope you'll wash your hair *before* you get into bed tonight having worn dirty panties on your head. No, it's about the bathroom floor.'

I'm confused. What crime am I supposed to have committed against the oatmeal limestone floor tiles?

'If you're going to stay here then we have certain rules in this house, and one of them is making sure that the bathroom floor is free of hairs after you've used it, *including* pubic hairs.'

I nearly fall off my chair with shock. I can certainly feel my cheeks burning with embarrassment.

'You left some of yours on the floor last night. It's understandable if you're using a towel, briskly.'

All I can think of gasping is, 'Are you sure they were mine?'

Bella nods. 'Oh, yes. My family are all blonde, and these ones were on the brown side.'

I can't believe it! The woman has obviously been on her hands and knees examining hair from my nether regions like she's some kind of genital detective.

'I'm sorry,' I mumble through a mouthful of rabbit food. 'I won't let it happen again.'

'It's not a problem, but just have a quick look round making sure that you pick any up with a wad of damp tissue which you can then flush down the toilet.'

I swallow the last of my breakfast and push back my chair hoping to escape, but Bella hasn't finished with me yet. I get more rules about always using coasters with mugs or glasses, rinsing things before putting them in the dishwasher, folding magazines and newspapers back to the front when I've finished with them, taking my outside shoes off at the front door, the list goes on and on. I think I lost consciousness around the time she told me that if I get up off the sofa and see I've squished a cushion, I should plump it up *immediately*.

I drift back to reality as Bella is saying, 'These are all tips you can take back home with you. You might like to share them with your mother.'

I want to get up but I can't move. I've lost the will to live and I'm scared that Bella will see that I've got my outside shoes on, inside.

'And whilst we're alone, do you want to talk about what I saw you doing last night?'

There are so many things I might have done which

would be a problem to The Neat Freak, it's difficult to know where to start.

'The self-harming?' Bella prompts.

What *is* she talking about?

'You were attacking yourself when Tom and I drove past. You can't deny it. We both saw you doing it.'

I can hardly say that I was hitting myself in the face to try and stop Dad going out with a woman who looks like a kipper, even if it is the truth, so I try to look as blank-faced as possible.

'Well, let's talk about it tomorrow. Perhaps after lunch? Let's say two-thirty back here at the kitchen table. I've already downloaded some information from the Internet for us to go through, together.'

As if, I think to myself.

Chapter Twenty-one

I stretch out in the warm sunshine, wriggle my toes and let out a deep sigh of happiness.

Despite the fact that I accidentally exposed my big, round, naked butt to The Spanish Lurve God, it's been a glorious day spent in the garden lying on sunloungers which are all padded, unlike the ones at our house which are thin, leave mesh marks all over your legs and sometimes spontaneously fold up, trapping your bum painfully in the hinge.

Tom, James and Jags are at golf, and Bella drove off to an antiques fair to get some home-stylist stuff. No one will be back until at least six o'clock. Bella told Lucy to carry on with her French, but like she's *so* going to do that whilst I'm here and it's sunny outside.

Luce seems much more relaxed now The Neat Freak has gone out. Seeing how she behaves around Bella it's obvious she finds her mum as much of a strain as I do. Everything and everyone has to be perfect in The Neat Freak's world, and it's exhausting.

I rang Sorrel and told her I was staying at Lucy's for the weekend because The Love Birds wanted me out of the way and did she want to come over? She had her own family problems as Ray was at the camera shop all day, Jas was working at New Look and sulky Senna is too young to babysit, so Sorrel had look after the twins until the lunchtime rush at The Bay Tree Café was over, after which she dumped them with Yolanda and came round.

We've been having a complete bitch-fest about the Queen Bee girls who gatecrashed my party, trying to work out who was doing what to whom, and whether Jags was doing anything to anyone, but particularly Tits Out once she'd finished necking Buzzer. Just in case sliding down Jags means that he'll never look at me again, I'd have liked to have assigned some S-Scores to the other King William boys who came, but I was too trashed to notice whether they were Gods or Trolls.

'Luce, are you sure the others won't be back for ages?' Sorrel asks.

'Positive,' Lucy replies.

'Well then . . .' She sits up, whips off her T-shirt and wriggles out of her denim mini-skirt so she's just sitting in her black bra and knickers.

'I can't believe you've just done that after what happened to me!' I shriek. 'What if they come back and see you in your scanties?'

'So what?' Sorrel lies back on the sunlounger. '*My* sacred bits are covered. *Yours* weren't.'

I can't risk another Bella episode, but I push my top right up, drag my T-shirt sleeves over my shoulders, and roll my skirt up to my thighs. I've changed my knickers so at least they now say *Saturday* if anyone gets an accidental flash.

'Come on, Luce, how about stripping off?' Sorrel says.

'I'm fine,' Lucy replies.

'Aren't you hot in that T-shirt?' I ask her.

'I'm sun aware, that's all.' She sounds a bit tense. 'I don't want to get dodgy killer moles.'

'Oh come on, Miss Prim,' Sorrel teases. 'It's summer! Show some skin for a change.'

'Get off me!'

I sit bolt upright, shocked by the snarl in Lucy's voice.

'What happened?' I've had my eyes closed so I'm squinting into the sunlight, but as I focus I can see Lucy standing up, hugging herself.

'I was just larking about!' Sorrel says. 'I just tried to pull her T-shirt off.'

'Well, I don't find it funny!' Lucy's close to tears. 'Not everyone wants to strip off at the drop of a hat!'

'Luce! Chill out!' Sorrel looks bewildered. 'I was only—'

'Just leave me alone, will you! Both of you!' she screams, running towards the house and slamming the back door behind her.

I can hear from Lucy's breathing that she's still awake, even though she probably wants me to think she's asleep. We've hardly spoken since her garden outburst. Sorrel and I ran after her but she shot up to her room and slammed that door too, making it crystal clear that she wanted to be left alone.

Sorrel was gutted and left. She still doesn't know what she did wrong and, to be honest, neither do I. I've known Luce for ten years and not once has she ever lost her cool like that.

I said I'd text Sorrel if I found out what was going on, but as Luce stayed in her room, I just sat in the sun, read magazines, made myself a drink and then spent the last half-hour before Bella was due home rushing around the house like a blue-arsed fly, making sure I couldn't be prosecuted for leaving a magazine open or letting a stray coffee cup escape the dishwasher.

It was weird Luce going off on one like that, but what was *really* weird was that the moment Bella's car pulled into the drive, Lucy appeared in the kitchen, all sunny blonde smiles as if nothing had happened. She told Bella she'd spent the day reading a French novel to which Bella exclaimed, '*Très bien!*'

For tea we had salade niçoise, which just looked like lettuce and a few smelly boiled eggs to me, and then Bella and Tom went to a neighbour's barbecue clutching a bottle of red wine.

James went to his room without even speaking to us, and Lucy and I watched a DVD of *Dirty Dancing* before going to bed, which is where we've been for the last hour, lying in tension-filled silence.

'You awake, Luce?' I whisper into the dark.

Nothing.

'Look, Luce. Is everything OK? You've been acting a bit, well, weird.'

Still nothing, but the thing about posh sheets is that they rustle, and from the rustling sound coming from Lucy's bed, I know she's awake and fidgeting.

'It's just that it's not like you to be mega-stroppy. That's more of a Sorrel or me thing.'

Silence.

'You know you can tell me anything, don't you?'

I give up. There's no point. Sorrel obviously pushed one of Lucy's panic buttons, but I'm not going to find out why tonight.

I bash my pillow a bit and snuggle down in the hope that I'll have a nice Jags dream, one where I'm not flashing my knickerless bits. Then I hear Lucy rolling over towards me.

'Would you tell me your deepest darkest most secret secret?' she whispers. 'Something you've never told anyone, *ever*.'

'Course I would,' I reply. 'But only if you told me something back.'

There's a long pause before Lucy says, 'Go on then. You first.'

This is going to be *really* difficult. I can hardly admit it to myself. But perhaps if Lucy knows my most disgusting stomach-churning humiliating secret, she might tell me what's bugging her.

I gulp. 'OK. Sometimes, when I'm dreaming about kissing Jags, his face changes and he turns into . . . Freak Boy!'

'No!' Lucy gives a whispery shriek. She's laughing so much I can hear her beating the mattress with her feet. 'You fantasize about snogging FB! I don't believe it.'

'Well, as soon as it happens I stop the fantasy,' I say,

beginning to wonder whether perhaps I should have made up a secret instead of telling the awful Freak Boy truth. 'I don't let him snog me once I realize it's him. I push him away or beat him about the head with a badminton racket.'

'Even so!' Lucy giggles. 'You've still fantasy-snogged Frazer Burns!'

'Go on then,' I say, trying to get off the Freak Boy subject before it gets even more humiliating. 'Your turn.'

Lucy doesn't say anything.

'Oh come on, Luce, spill the beans! You can't make me tell you my worst secret if you're not going to tell me yours.' I'm totally miffed that she's tricked me into one-sided secret spilling.

There's silence and I really think she's going to wimp out but then she says quietly, 'I do the same thing as you.'

'I don't believe it!' I gasp. 'You fantasy-snog Freak Boy too!'

I'm shocked. She's kept that one quiet! What is it about that beaky-freaky weirdo that gets people secretly fancying him? It's the eyes. It must be the eyes. He's got his dad's eyes. Perhaps he's using those sexy eyes to hypnotize us into fantasy-fancying him.

I shift up the bed, plump up my pillows and then remember I *still* haven't washed my hair, so spend a couple of seconds freaking out that Bella will sniff the sheets and realize.

'How far do you let him go before you become disgusted with yourself?' I ask her. I hadn't admitted to Lucy that sometimes I don't beat FB off with the badminton racket quite as quickly as I should.

'No, no, I didn't mean that.' Lucy's voice sounds tense and wobbly. 'Not that secret. The more secret secret. The bad one. The one Mum knows you do, but doesn't know I do, although I do, except I didn't know you did until I heard Mum say you do.'

I've got absolutely no idea what Lucy's gabbling about. She's obviously gone bonkers and the mega-strop was the first sign. Perhaps we all spent too much time lying in the sun and her brain has become scrambled. How much worse can a secret be than admitting you have nanoseconds of lustful thoughts about a freaky beaky alien, even if his cells *are* jam-packed with gorgeous DNA?

I can hear Lucy breathing heavily into the dark and then she starts sniffing.

'Luce?'

Something's wrong. The atmosphere in the room has changed from tense, to fun and then to mega tense.

I reach over and click on the bedside light, and after

I've blinked a bit, I see Lucy sitting up in bed, hugging her knees, tears streaming down her face.

'Lucy! What is it?' I get out of bed and go over to her. By now she's really sobbing, rocking backwards and forwards.

'What's wrong?'

I keep asking her what's wrong but she can hardly speak for sobbing and rocking. Whatever it is, it's obviously bigger than fantasy-snogging a freak.

'Is it your mum and dad? Are they splitting up or is one of them about to die or . . . ?'

She shakes her head and snot flies out of her nose on to the white sheets as she continues to rock backwards and forwards, gasping for breath.

'Oh, my God, is it you? Have you got a brain tumour or something? Is that why you've been acting well odd? Are you going to die?'

I burst into tears.

'No!' Lucy gasps. 'Nothing like that. I heard Mum talking to you in the kitchen. I was listening in the hall. She said she'd caught you harming yourself.' The words come out between gulps and sobs. 'She said that's what you were doing when she saw you on Friday.'

I feel so relieved that I was wrong about Lucy's brain tumour.

'I was slapping myself in the face to get The Kipper into

243

trouble,' I say, hugging her. 'Your mum got the wrong idea.'

'So you don't hurt yourself on purpose?'

'No, but Luce—'

'Forget I ever said anything.' She pushes me away. 'I was just worried about what I'd heard that's all. I was just worried for you.'

It's not all. I *know* it isn't.

Lucy leans over to turn out the bedside light but I grab her wrist.

'Let go!' she shrieks, trying to wrestle free, but salami limbs win over twiglets and the light stays on.

'Lucy, tell me!' I plead. 'Tell me what's going on.' I shake her wrist. 'I'm not going to let go until you do.'

She looks exhausted. Small. Scared. Defeated.

Finally she swings her legs over the side of the bed and, with a shaking hand, slowly lifts up her pyjama top.

I drop her wrist in shock.

Suddenly it all makes perfect sense.

Going mad at Sorrel for trying to pull her T-shirt up.

Never wearing little tops even in the baking heat.

Never going out with any of the boys that ask her for dates.

Running away from the woman in Top Shop last Easter who suggested Luce could be a model.

Not wanting me to share a room with her.

Criss-crossing her tummy is a tangled mass of white lines, pink scars and some fresh red wounds dotted with dried blood.

'They're on my back and shoulders too,' she whispers. 'Scratching myself is the only way I can cope with life.'

Chapter Twenty-two

I look at the bedside clock.

12.33 a.m.

Lucy is still talking, well, whispering really. We'd turned the light out about midnight when we heard Bella and Tom come in as Luce started stressing about them seeing the light under the door. It was only then, lying in the dark, head to tail in her bed, that Lucy opened up and told me *everything*.

It all came out in a torrent about how Bella's not just into neat freakery, but is a total control freak too, demanding ultimate perfection from her house, her hairdresser *and* her family. How she doesn't just go on and on about leaving pubes on the floor or insist that towels are hung up perfectly straight, but makes Luce keep her CDs in alphabetical order, won't let her put pictures up in her room unless they're framed and tasteful, and regularly checks her wardrobe to make sure it's organized by both style *and* colour.

'Sometimes, when something falls off a hanger I think, *So what?* and leave it there like a mini-rebellion,' Lucy says into the darkness. 'But then I keep thinking of it crumpled in the wardrobe and Mum finding out, and her lecturing me about a tidy house equalling a tidy mind, and I get so stressed I have to rush back and sort it out.'

'But your mum has always been like that and it never seemed to bug you,' I say. 'Why now?'

'Last October when Michael went up to uni, Mum started going on and on about how well James was doing at school and how fantastic it was that Michael had got into Imperial, and how if I didn't work harder I'd let the family down and end up on a park bench swigging meths.'

'Your mum said you'd become a trampy wino?' God, no wonder Lucy's screwed up.

'Well, she didn't actually say that,' Lucy admits, 'but she implied it. And then she said if I was going to have any chance of doing well at school she was going to have to take me away from Burke's and send me to Church Hill for Year 10. She's still hoping a place will come free over the summer and is planning ways of how I can get to the top of the waiting list.'

'But Church Hill is rubbish!' I say. 'Just private rubbish, miles away. I don't think they do any better in the league tables than we do.'

'I know. But it doesn't have . . .' Lucy stops herself.

'Doesn't have *what*?'

She says nothing.

'Oh come on, Luce, you've told me everything else.' I gently kick her in the bum. 'What does Church Hill have that Burke's hasn't, other than a better uniform?'

I hear her gulp. Several times.

'It doesn't have you and Sorrel. Mum thinks you're both bad influences on me. Particularly you and especially recently.'

'The bitch!' I shriek as Lucy hisses at me to keep quiet. 'Listen, Luce, I know it's bad form to call your mum a bitch, but she really is. You need to wear that T-shirt I got for my birthday.'

'She just wants the best for me,' Lucy sighs. 'She wants me to be the magazine-perfect daughter and I can't be that all the time. Sometimes *I* can't control things. You remember when you and Sorrel put all Mum's shoes in the wrong boxes on purpose?'

I do remember. We thought it would be a laugh to wind up The Neat Freak and rearrange her designer shoe collection, but it got Luce into shed-loads of trouble.

'Well, that's when it started. She told me she wanted to send me to Church Hill to get me away from you, so I ran up to my room and started shouting and sort of beating the hell out of my bed, and then Mum came in and began lecturing me about anger management and not breaking the goose feathers in the duvet. When she'd gone I wanted to shout and rip the bedding to bits, but knew I'd get another lecture if I did, so instead I ripped myself, on my arm, with my fingernails. It felt so good, like a sort of release.'

'But didn't she notice?' I ask, thinking of Bella with her eagle eye for anything that isn't perfect.

'Oh, yes, she noticed, but I said that Sorrel's cat had mauled me and she believed me. And then it felt brilliant to have a secret from her. It was something she couldn't control. Something she didn't know anything about. It was *my* thing and I could do it in places without anyone seeing. But it's become harder to hide in the summer. That's why I freaked when Sorrel tried to get me to strip. I thought you'd all notice. But it might have been better if you did because now it's got out of control and I'm scared.'

'But if Bella thinks I'm a bad influence on you, why did she invite me to stay?' I ask. 'Why did she put us in the same room? None of it makes sense.'

'She probably thinks she can change you,' Lucy says. 'You'll become one of her projects. She'll have you dressing in beige and stand over you while you floss your teeth every night, and before you know it you'll be a Malone clone.'

If deep snores equal deep sleep, then Luce slept really well, unlike me who crawled back into my bed about 2 a.m., and spent the next few hours tossing and turning in the crackly sheets. Perhaps it was unloading everything on to me that helped calm her. I'm glad for her, but now I feel like I've got the weight of several worlds pressing down on my meaty shoulders. I'm also mega-furious that Bella has been so two-faced, pretending to be nice to me whilst dissing me behind my back, plotting to either change me, or keep the two of us apart.

I glance across at Lucy who's fast asleep, looking completely angelic and perfect. No one would ever know that her head is so messed up she messes up her body. I certainly had no idea. None of us did. Perhaps if I hadn't been so stressy-headed about the whole Mum-Dad-Bitch-Troll-Kipper scene I might have noticed that my best friend was gouging great lumps out of her skin. I'd sometimes wondered whether Luce was a secret anorexic as she never seems to eat much and is so thin, but it turns out I was wrong. She's not into starving herself on purpose, just scratching herself until she bleeds.

I feel completely out of my depth. I don't know what to do. This is *way* too big for me to cope with. Scarily big. This isn't a normal everyday secret, it's a serious one, and I'm going to *have* to tell someone. What if Luce ends up in hospital with infected scars that ooze greeny-yellow pus and nearly dies from blood poisoning? Or what if she actually does die and then I say, 'Oh, yeah, I knew she was ripping herself to shreds but I did nothing about it because she told me not to.' But if I do tell someone Lucy will think I've betrayed her, and if she thinks she can't rely on me, the only person she's been able to talk to, that could make things a whole lot worse.

'Hi!' I say as Luce opens her eyes.

'What time is it?' she asks sleepily.

I glance at the clock. 'Nearly nine-thirty.'

'Oh no!' She jumps out of bed, races to the window and pulls up the blind. 'Mum will start one of her *You're wasting the best part of the day* lectures.'

As she turns away from me and slips out of her pyjama top I see the scars on her shoulders and back. Long red lines as if some wild animal has been clawing at her skin.

We can't deal with this by ourselves.

'Luce, you're going to have to tell someone other than

me about this,' I whisper. *'Please.'*

'No!' Lucy hisses. 'And you're not to either. You promised.'

I don't remember promising and tell her so.

'A secret's not a secret if you tell someone,' she snaps back. 'I trusted you. If you dare tell anyone, I'll *never* speak to you *ever* again.'

'This is a nice surprise,' Mum says as she reverses out of the Malones' drive. 'I didn't think you'd be back so soon.'

Nor did I, I think to myself.

I give a half-hearted wave to Bella and Lucy who are standing on the doorstep, though really I'd love to give a two-fingers sign to The Neat Freak for being horrible about me and making Lucy's life hell.

Luce was obviously stressed out that I might grass her up to her mum, and I couldn't stand being around two-faced Bella after what Lucy told me, so after an uneasy morning when I painted each of my nails a different colour whilst Lucy sat in her room and did her homework, and a tense lunch because Bella kept trying to ask us both questions in French and neither of us knew what on earth she was talking about, I'd suggested I might ring Mum to see if she could come and pick me up. Lucy and Bella seemed so relieved to be shot of me they were practically packing my bags for me, and I was so relieved to go I was waiting at the window, willing the silver car to pull up. Leaving early also got me out of the planned 2.30 p.m. kitchen table self-harm meeting with Bella.

'What did you get up to?' Mum asks.

'Not much,' I shrug. 'What about you?'

'We ate Pot Noodles and watched a DVD about big ice cubes in the sea and played table football!' Jack yells from the back of the car, drumming his feet on the back of my seat. 'Until my goalie's head fell off.'

'So, did Phil win?' I ask, feeling a bit guilty that I was responsible for the decapitation and that the superglue I'd used obviously wasn't strong enough to cope with headed Subbuteo footballs.

'Jack and I played football,' Mum says. 'Phil was on call over the weekend. I haven't seen him since Thursday.'

This is a surprise. I'd imagined Jack would be farmed out to the Finkelsteins so Mum and Phil could have the house to themselves.

'So if Phil wasn't there, why did you want me out of the way?' I whinge. 'And why didn't you ask why I was crying on Friday night?'

'I thought you'd tell me if you wanted me to know why you were upset, and I thought *you* wanted to go to Lucy's.'

'Only because I thought you didn't want me around.'

'I didn't!' squeaks Jack. 'I liked having Mum all to myself. She says we can get a rabbit and I'm going to call it Theo after the footballer!'

Mum leans over and pats my thigh which *totally* freaks me out, not because she's showing affection, but because it means there's only one hand on the steering wheel, and even with two her driving's erratic.

'I think we've all had a few crossed wires recently,' she sighs, hands back on the wheel. 'Shall we make a pact to try and talk to each other in future?'

I nod. It will be a bit weird talking to Queen of the Clams, but it's worth a try. I *really* need to talk to someone about Lucy. I'm so tempted to tell Mum, but if I do, she'll do the grown-up-parent thing and tell Bella, and then Lucy will never forgive me. If I tell Sorrel, Lucy is bound to find out and never forgive me. Tits Out is a definite no as it would be all round the school within half an hour and she'll claim she's done the self-harming bit herself. Butterface would just look blank, I can't stand even being in the same room as Tammy Two-Names, and anyway they'd tell Claudia who'd tell the school. Even if Jags was my boyfriend I couldn't tell him because he'd tell James and then James would tell Bella. I could talk to Buff Butler which would mean I could help Luce whilst interacting with academic eye candy, but he would probably have to tell The Teapot who would probably tell the Malones, and then we're back to Lucy never forgiving me. Even though I'm a cow to Phil, he's probably a good person to talk to, but he's so lurved up with Mum, he'd probably tell her and then it's the whole Bella and Lucy-never-forgiving-me routine again.

Whatever I do, whoever I tell, it seems to me that all conversations would end up with me losing the trust of my oldest best friend.

Mum flips the indicator and we turn left into Talbot Road.

What I need is to talk this over with someone who is totally reliable and not going to blab it all round school.

'Mum, can you drop off me here?' I ask.

She throws me a look which says she doesn't really trust me because she doesn't know what I'm up to.

'Honestly, Mum, it's OK. I'll be home soon. I *promise*. There's just someone I need to see.'

Chapter Twenty-three

'Can I come in? There's something I want to ask you.'

Freak Boy grabs Archie who's been barking like a loony, jumping up and down and snarling through the frosted half-glass since I rang the doorbell. FB looks flustered to see me standing on his doorstep on a Sunday afternoon.

'Do you want me to follow your dad again?' he asks. 'It's just that my ankle's still a bit sore to ride a bike.'

'No, no, nothing like that,' I say, following him and the dog through the house and into the kitchen.

Glam Doc and Hot Dad are sitting in the conservatory, reading the papers. They glance up as I come in, and Dunc the Hunk waves before burying himself back in the *Sunday Times*.

'Do you want something to drink?'

FB's obviously in a right state about me being in his kitchen, as he's opening and closing the fridge door again and again without getting anything out. I'm pretty impressed to see that there are several bottles of champagne chilling in there, but I don't think he's offering me a glass of champers at four o'clock in the afternoon.

'No, I'm fine,' I say, leaning against one of the units. 'Look, you know you didn't want me to say anything about what happened to your ankle? Would you have forgiven me if I had said something, you know, like betrayed you to The Teapot?'

'You haven't told Mr Thomson, have you?' FB keeps his eyes on the floor, but his voice is panicky, though I notice it's not quite as squeaky as I remember it.

'Course not! I'm not a sticky beak!'

'It's not going to matter soon anyway,' he says, sitting opposite me at a rather snazzy dark-granite breakfast bar. I could imagine myself sitting there, eating my Shreddies in the morning. 'Mum and Dad are seriously thinking of sending me somewhere else.'

'Oh no!'

I say this so quickly it shocks even me. Damage limitation is required. 'I mean, it would be a shame, given that your dad went to Burke's and he wants you to go there and he turned out OK, eventually, didn't he?' I'm gabbling and I know I am.

FB looks straight at me with eyes that are *so* like his

dad's I find myself blushing.

'Electra, what's wrong? Are you in some kind of trouble?'

I didn't mean to tell him. I wasn't going to mention any names. I was just going to ask him what he would do if *theoretically* someone he knew was hurting themselves, *deliberately*. Would he tell his mum? Their mum? A teacher? I was going to say a friend, but at the last minute I remembered he hasn't got any, so I left that bit out. But I ended up telling him that it was Lucy who was in trouble, but as I had been sworn to secrecy I couldn't tell anyone and didn't know what to do.

He was easy to talk to. He didn't butt in, or shriek, or look shocked. He just sat there listening whilst I told him *everything*, even bits that weren't Lucy-related but were about Dad and The Kipper, and Mum and The Impostor.

'You have to get Lucy help,' FB says when I've finished my sorry tale. 'You know that, don't you? This isn't something you can deal with on your own. It's not something Lucy can deal with on her own either.'

'But *you* don't want anyone to know you're being bullied,' I whisper. 'Why won't you let anyone help you?'

FB shrugs. It's not just his voice that's different. His shoulders seem a bit broader than I remember too, but then he's usually got them hunched as he scurries along with his head down.

'I might have to if things get worse over the summer holidays. At half-term Pinhead, Gibbo and Spud were hanging around the end of the avenue *every* day waiting for me. But this is different. Lucy's in real trouble and it's not something changing schools is going to help.'

'But who can I tell who will help her but won't tell her mum?' I ask. It's been good for me to talk to someone, but it's helped me, not Lucy.

FB nods towards the conservatory. 'Do you think Lucy might talk to Mum? She *is* a doctor.'

As Frosty the Penguin drones on and on about Romeo and Juliet, I stare out of the first-floor classroom window, looking at nothing in particular, my butterfly brain flitting from shallow questions such as *Why is that afternoons in school go more slowly than afternoons at home?* to more serious issues, such as the fact that my best friend is ripping herself to shreds, and so far I've done absolutely nothing to stop her. Neither Lucy nor me have said anything about the weekend, though Sorrel asked if I'd found anything out about why Luce freaked. I just said I thought she was irritable with really bad PMT.

'Tell Lucy if she feels comfortable about it to give me a

ring anytime,' Glam Doc Fiona Burns had said as she'd written *F. Burns* and her moby number down on a piece of thick cream paper. 'She's welcome to come here for a coffee and a chat.'

'And you won't ring her mum?' I'd asked. After the first wave of relief that I'd told someone, particularly a proper tax-paying seriously grown-up someone who just happens to be a doctor, came a sort of sick churning feeling that even though I'd done it for the right reasons, I'd still betrayed my best friend.

'Not if I can help it but, when she's ready, I'll encourage her to tell her mother. I'd like to know if something was troubling my child.'

At that point I'd shot FB a knowing look, but he was tracing patterns on the granite worktop with his finger and didn't look up. I remember thinking that perhaps I should have made a deal with him such as *I'll tell Luce to talk to your mum if you tell your mum you're being bullied*, but I didn't, and now we're back at school there's no way I'm going to be seen communicating with Freak Boy.

I look at the bit of paper. I've looked at it so often I know Doc Burns's moby number off by heart. Just over three days I've carried it around with me. Three days when I've done nothing with it except constantly stare at it, fold it into a paper aeroplane, unfold it and stare at it again. Three days during which time Lucy could have clawed more bits of skin off her beautiful bod. The problem is I feel paralysed, as if I'm in some sort of holder-of-a-terrible-secret limbo. Scared to do something with the phone number. Too scared not to. But time is running out. Today is Thursday and term ends tomorrow lunchtime, and then Lucy will be with Bella The Control Freak for six weeks, including two weeks in France without Sorrel and me to dilute the tension. The thought of being holed up in some foreign country with Bella makes even *me* want to go mad, though I have to admit it's more because I'm still nuclear furious with her for thinking I'm a bad influence on Lucy, rather than the fact she seems to be at the root of her daughter's problems.

My daydreaming is rudely interrupted by the smell of rank BO and a pair of gnarled, swollen, sweaty, nylon-enclosed trotters standing beside me.

It's Frosty the Penguin.

'But, soft! what light through yonder window breaks?' she asks.

I stare up at her. The woman is clearly deranged and obviously needs the long summer holiday more than I do. Perhaps the smell of her own BO has sent her mental.

'O Electra, Electra, wherefore art thou Electra?' Frosty asks, and the class roar with laughter.

261

I've no idea why Frosty seems to be giving me a love speech from *Romeo and Juliet*, but that's just *so* typical of my luck. Instead of some totally lush teacher like Buff Butler falling for me, I've caught the eye of a wrinkly smelly penguin with lesbionic tendencies.

Mrs Frost leers over me. 'In other words, Electra Brown, your body might be sitting in my English class, but your brain, if you have one, is clearly somewhere else!'

I guess that means she doesn't fancy me then.

The Penguin spots Glam Doc's note. It's in its paper aeroplane phase of the folding and unfolding sequence, and looks like it's ready to be launched straight off the cover of one of Billy Boy Shakespeare's greatest works.

Like some sort of hawk after a defenceless mouse, she swoops down, grabs the note and opens it.

'This seems to be Frazer Burns's phone number,' she sneers. 'If you and Frazer want to organize your love lives, I suggest you do it in your own time.' She crumples the note into a ball and throws it back at me to gasps and sniggers.

As Frosty waddles back to the front of the class, I seriously contemplate hurling myself through the plate-glass window.

* * *

I'm out of the classroom, down the corridor and into the loos quicker than anyone can say *Freak Boy Lover!*

I need time to think.

Time to come up with a plausible explanation as to why I was sitting in English, staring out of the window, and in possession of a piece of paper on which *appeared* to be written Freak Boy's moby number.

I close a cubicle, sit on a toilet seat, and put my feet up on the door which is covered in marker-pen graffiti.

I can hear girls coming in and out. It's geography next which means there'll be some serious make-up reapplication in preparation for what could be the last lesson *ever* with Buff Butler.

No one will bother to bang on the door. They'll just think it's one of the bingeing barfing bulimics chucking up the three Twix and two Flakes they've stuffed into their mouths the moment the bell for break went. I'll stay here until the next bell goes and then just shoot straight into class without talking to anyone.

On the other hand, why don't I just tell a half-truth and say that the number was actually for Doctor Fiona Burns – the true bit – but I had it because I've got something wrong with me – the lie bit. It's a good half-lie, but I'll need to make sure that whatever is wrong with me isn't something horrid and contagious. I don't want someone writing *Electra Brown has VD* on the loo door in red marker pen as they've done with *Julie 'The Y11 Bike' Sneddon*. Perhaps I could just get away with a knowing look and a low whisper of 'Period troubles'.

I've just decided that this is a truly brilliant solution, combining as it does the truth but with a lie that is utterly convincing and plausible, when I hear Lucy's voice.

'Electra? You in there?'

No point in hiding now I know that I've got period troubles and a doctor to cure them, so I slide my feet down the door, get off the loo and come out of the cubicle.

There's so much hair littering the sinks from where everyone has been busy brushing and combing and primping you could knit a jumper for a fat hamster but, other than Lucy, the loos are now empty.

'You *are* in here!' she says, and begins to giggle. 'So, you're about to stop fantasy-snogging FB and do the real thing!'

'No way!' I hiss. 'That wasn't Freak Boy's moby number.'

'Don't worry, your snogging secret is safe with me!' Lucy says, and I feel a stab of guilt that *her* secret wasn't safe with me.

'No, honestly it wasn't!' I say. 'It's his mum's, Doctor Fiona Burns's.'

'Of course.' Lucy nods and eyes me in a way which leaves me in no doubt that she doesn't believe me. 'It's perfectly normal to carry around her number.'

I'm about to start the whole gynaecological lie when I realize that I can no longer wimp out. This is my chance to help Lucy.

I check there really isn't anyone in the loos, rummage in my bag and get out the crumpled note.

'It's not for me, Luce, it's for you. FB's mum said she'd help you, you know, with the whole self-harm thing. FB suggested it.'

The paper is rustling and I realize that my hand is shaking as I hand the note to Lucy. I try to use my other hand to steady my arm at the elbow, but both arms are shaking so I look a bit like I'm about to have some sort of fit.

Lucy looks shocked. 'You told Frazer Burns?' she says slowly, her eyes cold and wide. '*You* told Frazer Burns *my* secret even though you promised not to tell *anyone*?'

'Luce, I had to!' My voice is squeaky and hoarse. 'This is way too big for us to cope with on our own! Please!'

Lucy glares at me. Now my whole body feels shaky. Perhaps I *am* going to have a fit. Perhaps the stress of all this has sent my blood pressure so high my body's about to explode. Maybe there's some dodgy blood vessel in my brain which will burst with the extra pressure. Perhaps I'm going to die in order to save Lucy, though I really don't fancy taking my last breath on the loo floor as it's filthy.

As I don't seem to have collapsed in a dribbling heap, and Luce shows no sign of taking the phone number, I push it into her bag.

'How could you?' she snarls. 'I trusted you!' She swings round towards the door, and as she does so her long blonde hair hits me on the cheek with a stinging slap. 'Just leave me alone.'

The bell starts ringing for the next lesson and I grab my bag and rush out of the door to follow her.

The corridor is bursting with pupils streaming towards classrooms, and I have to elbow and barge my way through the crowd.

I can see Lucy ahead of me, her blonde head bobbing along at top speed.

We're just at the door to the geography room when I catch up with her, dragging her to a stop by her arm.

'Luce, please!' I plead, gasping for breath. 'It's for the best, honestly.'

'The best?' she screams, wriggling free of my grip which isn't as strong as it usually is because of the shaky arms. 'The best? I didn't tell *anyone*, not even Sorrel, that you've been snogging Frazer for ages. And yet *you* couldn't keep your big mouth shut.'

'I only snog Freak Boy in my dreams!' I shout back. 'It was fantasy-snogging!'

'You told him about me just to get in with him!' she snaps. 'You used me!'

'That's *so* not true!' I say. '*You* were the one who said sometimes you have to be a sticky beak. It was *you* who wanted me to tell Tosser Thomson about FB being bullied by The Grim Reaper and his gang!'

'Oh, go to hell!' Lucy snaps.

And then she's off, running down the corridor.

There's jeering coming from the classroom, and I look in to see Sorrel glaring at me, Buff Butler staring at me, and Claudia and her slaggy friends laughing at me.

To chants of 'Electra snogs Razor! Electra snogs Razor!' Freak Boy darts out of the classroom, his face beety red, and starts to half run and half limp down the corridor.

What *have* I done?

Chapter Twenty-four

'If there's something wrong with your breathing then perhaps you need to see Dr Chaudhri,' Mum says as I sit slumped at the kitchen table. 'Shall I telephone the surgery?'

The looking glassy-eyed on the sofa plan hasn't worked, so to force everyone into realizing just how bored I *really* am, I've been sitting at the kitchen table trying the serial deep-sigh technique. Annoyingly, instead of getting the hint that I'm dying of terminal boredom, it's obvious Mum thinks I've developed asthma and am simply gasping for breath.

I've been bored rigid for over two weeks, ever since school finished.

To cheer me up I'd been hoping for an all-expenses-paid trip to see the Wundercousin in New York or, failing that, a shopping spree at Eastwood Circle to buy me a new iPod, but there's no sign of any MP3 hardware from Mum *or* Dad, and the only hint of a holiday is possibly a few days with Grandma and Granddad Stafford which is *so* not the sort of break I had in mind. Mum and Grandma always end up having a row because Grandma can't stop herself going on and on about how wonderful Aunty Vicky's family is, Granddad takes himself off to the shed to fiddle with bits of wood, and I'm left to play dinosaurs or Top Trumps with The Little Runt.

What's made the whole lack-of-holiday scenario even worse is that Dad rang and told me that he's going to Spain with The Kipper in September.

'Caroline said it was such a shame that the only dates available were after you'd gone back to school, otherwise you could have come with us,' Dad had said in a way which leads me to believe he's falling hook, line and lying stinker for her two-faced plan. I'm tempted to bunk off school and turn up at the airport as a nasty surprise. I bet the sight of me with my sun hat and flip-flops would drain the colour out of her bony orange face.

I've been making the days seem shorter by sleeping late but, annoyingly, Phil had the bad manners to start cutting the grass this morning which woke me up ridiculously early at ten o'clock.

'What's wrong is that I am B.O.R.E.D. Bored,' I say, throwing myself over the table in a suitably melodramatic fashion. I then do start to gasp uncontrollably because someone has left a crushed Shreddie on the table and I've snorted up a pile of toasted wheat.

'Oh, for goodness' sake, Electra,' Mum says, loading the dishwasher and ignoring the fact that I'm dying from breakfast cereal inhalation rather than boredom. 'You spend all year moaning about how you don't want to go to school, and then the moment you get some time off, you moan about how you've got nothing to do. When are the girls back from holiday?'

I blow my nose on a bit of kitchen roll – gross, as bits of brown Shreddie and snot come out – and shrug.

I've told Mum that I haven't seen or heard from the girls because they're both away on holiday, but it's a lie. I can't tell her the real reason they're both blanking me by not returning my calls, my texts or even acknowledging the card I sent Lucy which had a cute-looking bear with a tear in its eye saying *Sorry*. If I do, then I'll have to tell her about Lucy and the fingernails, and then Mum will be straight on the phone to The Neat Freak and Luce will be doubly-bummed at me. On the other hand as I've already lost Lucy as a friend, perhaps I might as well go for it and tell Mum anyway, especially as I'm not only bored, I'm worried about what Lucy is up to, stuck at home with Bella.

As I betrayed her, I can understand Lucy deleting me from her life, but Sorrel has too, though I don't know why. Luce didn't come back to school for the last day of term and neither did Sorrel. Everyone did the usual stuff of writing on each other's shirts and throwing flour bombs around, but it wasn't the same without them. I missed them then, and I miss them even more now.

'Why don't you go and look round the shopping centre?' Mum suggests. 'You might see one of your other friends there.'

I roll my eyes. I can't go and mooch around Eastwood Circle in case I'm spotted and ridiculed as the girl who snogs Freak Boy, ditto the sports centre, the newsagent's or anywhere within a ten-mile radius of Mortimer Road.

I am officially Electra No Mates.

Phil comes into the kitchen with leaves and twigs stuck to his head from where he's had to bend under the trees to cut the lawn. With his stubbly beard and foliage accessories he looks like a tramp whose been sleeping rough, rather than sleeping in Mum's bed. No one has actually said anything about this new development, but he's been downstairs when I've gone to bed and he's still here in the morning and the sofa bed is still covered in junk. I'm not a kid. I know what's going on.

Checking that the surface is free from snortable debris, I throw myself back across the table (still pock-marked with cigarette burns) and give an extra-loud, deep sigh.

'Still bored?' Phil asks.

At least he realizes I'm bored rather than suffering from respiratory failure.

I go to nod but forget that my head is already resting on the table and crack my nut on the pine.

'Well, ring Sorrel,' he says, washing his hands as I rub my forehead and curse under my breath. 'She must be back from holiday. I saw her outside her mum's café late yesterday afternoon.'

'I've tried but I think there's something wrong with her moby,' I lie.

'Well, let me have a quick coffee and then I'll run you over there,' he says.

I tried to say I didn't want a lift and that I'd do my own thing, but then Mum got all stressy and said I either went out and saw Sorrel, or I'd have to do some housework such as tidying The Little Runt's room whilst he's out at summer soccer school. So as the choice was between touching toxic clothes and toys or going to Sorrel's, I chose Sorrel's, even though I'm not actually sure how I'm going to get home without someone from my year seeing me and humiliating me in public.

'It's OK, you can go now,' I say to Phil as he pulls up outside Sorrel's house.

What with calling all her children after herbs and being into alternative living, I expect Yolanda would have liked to live in a cottage with honeysuckle round the door and a camomile lawn, but number 5 Forge Road is at the end of a row of modern terraced houses, each fronted by a strip of tarmac. Everyone has a car or two parked on the drive, except number 5, which is a jungle of pots with herbs and flowers, and a sundial outside the green front door.

'I'll just wait until you make sure she's in,' Phil says as I scramble out muttering 'Thanks' under my breath.

I wave at him, first in a friendly *Goodbye* type of way, and then in an unfriendly *Go away* type of way, but *still* he sits there. I can't wait to pass my driving test. I'm so fed up of having lifts and then being spied on. Can't these people just drop and go?

I'll just have to creep up the path, stand at the front door, pretend to knock on it and then when no one answers hot-foot it back to the car and say everyone was out.

I tiptoe through the pots of lettuces, go up to the front door with its *Face Food Free Zone* notice and, just as I'm about to pretend to knock on it, it opens and a black and white cat streaks past me and heads out into the road.

'Yeah?' A sullen-faced girl with milk-bottle glasses and wiry hair glares out from between the wind chimes, crystal mobiles and dreamcatchers hanging in the doorway.

It's Senna, Sorrel's younger sister. She always looks as if she's in a seriously bad mood, but I guess if your mother has run out of nice herb names and lands you with one known as a laxative, it kind of blights your life from birth.

'Is Sorrel in?' I ask, half hoping she isn't and half hoping she is.

'She's out,' Senna growls, as the twins, Sorrel's identical half-brothers Orris and Basil Johnson, race down the hallway and peer round her vast jean-clad hips. For a ten-year-old she has *very* wide hips, but I suppose they match her vast ass.

OJ and BJ are cute. They've got blond curly hair, cappuccino-coloured skin and sunny four-year-old smiles which sadly only makes the constipation kid look even more of a scowly bad-tempered lump.

'No, she's not,' pipes up one of the twins, giggling.

'She's hiding in the kitchen,' says the other. 'She hid when we saw you tiptoeing up the path!'

Senna biffs each of them around the head, so they slap her back.

'It's OK,' a voice calls out from deep within the house.

Sorrel comes down the hall towards me.

She shoves past her sister and brothers, barks at Senna to keep the twins away, and crouches on a step in the doorway. I'm not sure whether it's a friendly type of crouch, or an *About to spring into life and scratch my eyes out* type of crouch. Either way I'm on my own, as with a toot of the horn Phil *finally* pulls away.

I sit cross-legged on the ground next to her. I'm not sure I've chosen a good spot as I'm right beside a plant pot of something smelly which is attracting masses of bees, and I'm starting to get stressy that I might be attacked by a swarm of stingy winged things.

For a few moments we sit in the sunshine, in silence; well, silence other than the sound of Senna screaming at the twins who are now yelling, the bees revving up their stinging gear to attack me, and the whine of lawnmowers from the surrounding gardens.

Then we both say at the same time, 'Have you heard from Luce?'

I shake my head. 'I've phoned her and texted her and even sent her a card, but nothing. You?'

To my surprise, Sorrel nods. 'She sent me a text to say she just wanted to have some time on her own and she'd be in touch, but she hasn't. Do you know what's bugging her?'

I nod. 'I do, but I can't tell you. I'm sorry if that bums you.' I shuffle away from the bee magnet as the winged things sound as angry as Sorrel looks.

'I'm bummed you shared Lucy's secret with Freak Boy, not me. And I'm narked that you told Lucy about you and him and not me,' she says. 'You didn't share *anything* with me.'

'There is no me and Freak Boy,' I say. 'Luce wasn't going to tell me her secret, but after she freaked in the garden that day, I had to tell her something to get her to spill the beans so I made something up about FB.'

'So you haven't snogged him?'

'As if!'

'But why did you tell that freak and not me?' Sorrel asks. '*I'm* your friend, not that weirdo.'

'It just felt the right thing to do,' I say. 'I'm sorry.'

'And you're not going to tell me what's wrong with Lucy?'

I shake my head. 'I can't. But Luce will tell you when she's ready. I know she will.'

'That's cool,' Sorrel says, breaking into a smile. 'At least I know I can trust you if anything mad or bad happens to me. The worst you'll do is tell that freak but as no one speaks to him but you, that's OK.'

'What are we going to do about Lucy?' I ask.

'I think we should go round,' says Sorrel.

I'm not so sure. 'She probably won't answer the door if she sees I'm there,' I say.

'Well, I did,' Sorrel replies, getting up off the step. 'Let me dump these kids on a neighbour and let's go and give it a try.'

Chapter Twenty-five

We went by bus as I felt it was OK to be seen in public as long as Sorrel was there to protect me from any snidey Freak Boy Boyfriend remarks but, as it turned out, I didn't see *anyone* I knew, probably because everyone else has been whisked away on exotic holidays by their parents.

We formulated a battle plan on the way there. We decided that it might be best if I kept out of the way until Lucy came to the door, and then Sorrel could suss out the scene and the tension level and decide whether the time is right for me and Luce to make up. So whilst Sorrel rings the bell, I'm crouching on the drive outside *Foxgloves*, hiding behind the right wing of Bella Malone's silver Beast Car.

The Neat Freak opens the front door with a big fake smile which collapses when she sees it's Sorrel.

There's quite a bit of conversation going on but, annoyingly, I'm too far away to hear it. I'm just wondering whether I can risk shuffling round the wing and towards the front bumper when, 'ARGHH!'

I'm hit up the backside and sent sprawling across the drive as around me legs and arms and bits of bike collide. I check that I'm still alive, remove the tennis racket from my head and stagger to my feet. I don't know whether to rub my chin which has been exfoliated by the block paving, or my bum which has had a bicycle tyre shoved up it.

Not just any old bicycle tyre.

A Jags bicycle tyre.

He's lying amongst the last of The Neat Freak's black dahlias, groaning, his bicycle on top of him, its back tyre spinning.

I've killed The Spanish Lurve God or at the very least maimed him! I'll never get to snog him, or marry him, and the only reminder I'll have is a tyre mark on my butt. I wonder if I can photograph my own backside as a memento of being near him?

Bella and Sorrel rush over as James drags his friend to his feet shouting at me, 'What the hell were you doing hiding under our car? We had no time to brake!'

Much to my relief, other than dahlia juice on his tennis

whites and bits of mud clinging to his gelled hair, Jags is fine, his beautiful face unmarked, unlike mine which is stinging and, from the look of the finger I've used to check out the chin damage, bleeding.

Bella doesn't bother to ask if I'm all right.

'I thought Lucy was with you?' she says. 'Hasn't she been at yours all day?'

'I haven't seen her since school broke up.' I lick chin-blood off my finger.

'Don't be ridiculous, Electra. Lucy's been round at your house or Sorrel's every day for over two weeks.' There's a pause. 'Hasn't she?'

I shake my head.

'Sorrel?' Bella demands.

Sorrel shakes her head too.

Bella's face is a picture as it dawns on her that her perfect daughter has been feeding her porky pies.

Jags is still standing there looking ruffled but gorgeous. There's no score higher than 5 on the Snogability Scale, but I may have to seriously consider increasing it to 6, especially as both Hot Dad and Buff Butler's scores keep creeping up.

'I saw your kid sis when we left the tennis courts,' Jags says, examining his bike wheel which looks terminally twisted. 'She was walking along Talbot Road.'

'When? How long ago?' Bella is manic. Even her perfect blonde bob seems to be bouncing uncontrollably.

'Not long,' Jags says. 'She was with that freaky beaky boy that bust his ankle. I saw her around there yesterday too.'

I suppose Bella could have waited for Lucy to come home and then barrage her with questions, but that's not The Control Freak's style. She wanted to know *where* Lucy was, and she wanted to know *now*, and as Luce wasn't answering her phone there was nothing for it but to lock up the house, order James, me, Jags and Sorrel into the Beast Car, and hurtle towards the area of the last-known Lucy sighting.

As Jags was the last one to see Lucy, he's been ordered to sit in the front, so instead of being sturdy-thigh-to-Spanish-thigh with The Lurve God, I'm wedged next to Sorrel who's in the middle next to James. Not only that, I'm sitting directly behind Jags, and as the headrest is really high I can't even see him. It's probably just as well as I had a sneaky look in my handbag mirror and my chin looks as if someone has taken a cheese grater to it.

We've done about three laps of Talbot Road and the surrounding streets when I spot Lucy, on her own, walking along Priory Gardens back towards the main road. I feel an unexpected and rather disturbing wave of relief that FB isn't with her.

Bella brakes so hard I'm glad I've buckled up in the back or I'd be hurtling into Jags. Pulling his clothes down is one thing, but decapitating The Spanish Lurve God is quite another and would *definitely* end any possible chance of romance between us.

'What on earth's been going on?' Bella shrieks as she leaves the car like a heat-seeking missile. Lucy looks shocked, as anyone ambushed on the street by a mad mother followed by four teenagers might be. 'Why have you been telling me you've been at Electra's when you haven't?'

I notice Luce takes several deep breaths and starts rhythmically tapping her thighs with her hands.

'Because I didn't want you to know that I've been seeing someone.' She sounds very calm.

'I knew it!' Bella cries. 'You've been seeing a boy! I can't believe you didn't share this with me! When can I meet him? What do his parents do? You do remember our talks on contraception?'

'Oh, back off, Mum,' James snaps. 'That's *why* she didn't tell you. To avoid all this or you giving us any more weird sex instructions with toys getting it on.'

'You had that too?' Lucy asks him. 'I had a teddy and my rag doll.'

'You got off lightly,' James replies. 'I had an Action Man and a robot so I was well confused.'

Everyone laughs except Bella who's standing stony-faced in shades of beige.

My laughing is hiding the fact that I'm pretty freaked to find out that Lucy has obviously been seeing FB, and even more freaked that I feel *really* jealous.

Bella looks put out.

'Well, let's carry this conversation on at home, Lucy. I'm not discussing it in the street, and Marjorie Whelan is coming round for afternoon tea. I want you to show her how you're coming along in French.'

Bella heads for the car and we start to amble after her. As I'm so close to home, I might stay here. I've a feeling Bella will keep an eye on Lucy in the front which means Jags will be in the back and, as thrilling as that seemed at first, the image of my already large thighs spread out on the black leather next to him is not a good one, plus I could really do with not sitting down as my backside is starting to ache from its tyre encounter.

'Who's Marjorie Whelan?' Lucy asks.

'Lucy, I've told you again and again she was coming for tea on Tuesday.' Bella sounds exasperated. 'Marjorie is Veronica Freeman's sister. Veronica is the headmistress of Church Hill. I'm hoping that if you make a good impression on Marjorie, she'll tell her sister what an asset you'd be to the school, and Mrs Freeman will push you to the top of the waiting list. We should have stuck to our guns and sent you there at least a year ago.'

Lucy stops walking and starts her deep-breathing and thigh-tapping routine. 'I've told you, Mum, I'm not going to Church Hill.'

'Nonsense,' Bella says breezily. 'In the car, everyone! We'll discuss this at home.'

'No we won't. We'll discuss it here.'

'Lucy?' Bella has a warning tone in her voice. I'm convinced that Luce will crumple and revert to her normal dutiful-daughter mode, but she stands firm, breathing and tapping, breathing and tapping.

'I'm not going to Church Hill and that's final.'

Bella looks cornered. There's nothing for it but for her to lash out like a wounded animal.

'Well, Lucy, I'm sorry to have to say this in public, but you *are* going to Church Hill because, as you well know, the reason you have to leave Flora Burke's is because your friends, particularly Electra, are bad influences on you. I can't have you entering your first GCSE year surrounded by damaged people.'

Sorrel and I shoot looks at each other. We both want to shoot Bella.

'Electra, I know you and your family have issues now you're from a broken home, issues which I feel can be resolved by a programme of family counselling, personal rehabilitation and a good cleaning lady. But until your mother faces up to the problems I can't have you harming my daughter's education. What with the lies, the drinking and the self-harming, you are *not* a good role model for someone like Lucy.'

'I wasn't harming myself!' I almost shout at Bella. 'I was only hitting myself in the face because I was being victimized by The Kipper and I wanted to get her into trouble!'

'That's her dad's latest tart,' Sorrel explains. 'Was that before or after you gobbed on her poppadom?'

'See what I mean!' Bella shrieks. 'What sort of a girl spits on food and then whacks herself about the face?'

She looks round at all of us as if she's wanting someone to reply.

'The sort that pulled my Calvins down when she was wasted?' Jags suggests, which was *so* unhelpful, though I'm pleased he realized it was me, and it finally answers the question of what happened outside my bedroom door, though not what went on inside it.

'Exactly!' Bella is triumphant that someone, even a gorgeous but snitchy Spanish Love Rat, agrees with her.

285

'Electra, on a personal level I'm very fond of you and always have been, but the fact remains, as you have grown up you have become a negative influence on my daughter!'

'Stop it!' Lucy says firmly. 'Stop it at once, Mum. My friends are *not* a bad influence on me. *You* are. You're suffocating me!'

Bella looks as if a wasp has flown into her mouth and she's sucking on it.

Now Lucy's started there's no stopping her.

'I am not going to Church Hill. I want to be able to put up posters even if they're not stylish and in frames. It's not the end of the world if once in a while I leave a mug in my bedroom or a CD out of its case, and I don't want to go on holiday to France if it's just a chance for you to force me to speak French all the time.'

I'm mega impressed that Lucy is sounding calm and hasn't turned into the sort of screeching banshee I know I'd become if I was setting out a list of grievances to my mum.

'Last year you got me to go into a chemist and ask for a pack of Tampax. Every time I didn't say it perfectly you'd go "Encore" and I'd have to say it again. I ended up with ten packets which was *so* embarrassing!'

'But you needed the practice!' Bella says. 'You need to

be prepared for any medical emergency.'

'Since when were itchy bum-grapes an emergency?' James asks. 'I was ten years old and I was sent in to buy pile ointment!'

'Your father's haemorrhoids were playing him up and he was grumpy,' Bella shouts, just as someone walks past with their dog. 'Look, it's obvious you think I'm the worst mother in the world when all I've ever tried to do is be the best mother imaginable!'

I can tell Bella is finding it a struggle not to cry.

Lucy goes over to her mum and puts an arm around her.

'Look, Mum, I love you, we all do, but you've got to stop trying to control everything. There's a difference between controlling and guiding, and you're always trying to control me.'

'All of us,' James adds.

'You're a fantastic mum because you want the best for us,' Lucy says. 'But we're not little kids any more. Don't lecture us. Try listening to us instead.'

'Well, I'll try,' Bella sniffs. 'Are you coming home now?'

'What time is Mrs Sister of the Headmistress coming round?'

'Four o'clock,' Bella says. 'But if you'd rather not . . .'

We all look at our watches. Just after two. I'm bummed

to see that it's not only my face that was grazed in the bike collision, the face of my watch is scuffed too.

'I'll just hang out with the girls for a bit, but I'll be back, even though I'm not leaving Burke's and I'm not pouring tea with a French accent.'

'Could you take me to The Bay Tree, Mrs M?' Sorrel asks Bella. 'It would really piss Mum off if you could drop me off in the Beast Car.'

Bella nods. 'Boys? You coming?'

Sorrel sits in the front beaming, and James and Jags climb in the back, and the silver tank pulls away.

'My house?' I suggest and Lucy nods.

As we begin to walk towards Mortimer Road I notice she's shaking.

'You OK?' I ask, taking her hand. Even though it's a warm summer's day, it's cold and clammy.

'Phew. Yes. It was the first time ever I've stood up to Mum calmly, but it helped that I'd been through it all before in theory. Fiona said I'd have to put everything we talked about into practice eventually. I just didn't realize it would happen so soon.'

'You've been seeing Doc Burns?'

So that's where Lucy has been going! She hasn't been secretly spending time with FB, she's been with his mother! I feel relieved that she's getting help and also, worryingly, that she's not going out with Freak Boy, not that I ever thought she'd be in his league anyway.

'Yes, just about every day since school broke up. She's fantastic. Really easy to talk to. I can tell her all the things I want to say to Mum without her going off on one or getting all stressed out. She's given me coping mechanisms and got me writing a feelings diary; well, not really a diary, more like lots of letters to Mum explaining how I feel, although I'll never let her see them. I don't want to hurt her.'

'And it's helping?' I ask.

'Definitely. I've still a long way to go, but I feel I'm getting back a bit of my life,' Lucy replies. 'It's going to be tough going home after all this, but it feels better knowing James feels the same way.'

'And FB? You see FB too?' I have to ask. After all, Jags saw them together.

'Yes, I've been talking to Frazer too. In fact, when you and I had that row, he followed me out of school and made me see that I *had* to talk to someone. He's really lovely once you get to know him, and you were right, his dad's way up there on your S-Scale.' Lucy starts to giggle.

'Sorrel knows you have a secret,' I say. 'What are you going to tell her?'

'When the time is right, the truth,' Lucy replies. 'I know I can trust her.'

I feel stung. This is obviously directed at me. The best friend who couldn't keep a secret.

'I'm sorry,' I say, 'I just wanted—'

'To help me. I know.' She squeezes my arm. 'Frazer told me how scared you were for me. I didn't appreciate you being a sticky beak at the time, but now I do.'

A horn hoots and a silver car shoots past in the middle of the road.

It's Mum with her arm waving out of the window.

As we turn into Mortimer Road she's already parked up and the front door is open.

Jack gets out of the back of the car, still in his football gear, carefully holding a box punched with holes.

'Theo's come home!' he beams as we get level with the car.

He opens the box and Lucy and I peer in. Quivering in the hay is a tiny black rabbit.

'Oh, soo cute!' Lucy coos as Jack takes Theo into the house. 'I'd love a pet but Mum won't have one unless it does perfumed ready-wrapped poos!' Lucy's laughing and I realize I haven't seen her look so happy for months. 'I know you miss your dad, Electra, but honestly, you're so lucky, not just about Theo, about *everything*. Your mum's lovely and there are worse potential stepdads than Phil. He's a sweetie.'

I look at Mum who's come back down the steps with Phil. When he sees us he grins and gives us both a big wave and starts to help Mum unload bags of shopping from the boot of the car.

'Hello, Lucy love!' Mum says, trying to hug Lucy but managing to whack her with a combination of shopping bags and boobs. 'Fancy a cup of tea? I've bought cake!'

'Yes, please, but I've got to be back by four, so just a quick slice,' Lucy says, taking a bag from Mum and going into the house.

I watch Mum unload the last of the shopping.

She's got well-dodgy sunglasses on and is wearing the most hideous yellow strappy top and beige shorts. Every time she bends into the boot of the car her boobs swing forward, her knickers ride up and her belly flops over the top of her waistband. I think of Bella with her tight tummy and personality to match.

As Mum slams the car boot I lean forward and give her a kiss.

'Good heavens! Affection from my daughter!' she laughs. 'What have I done to deserve that?'

'Just for being you,' I say. 'That's all.'

About the Author

Helen Bailey was born and brought up in Ponteland, Newcastle-upon-Tyne. Barely into her teens, Helen invested her pocket money in a copy of *The Writers' and Artists' Yearbook* and spent the next few years sending short stories and poems to anyone she could think of. Much to her surprise, she sometimes found herself in print. After a degree in science, Helen worked in the media and now runs a successful London-based character licensing agency handling internationally renowned properties such as Snoopy, Dirty Dancing, Dilbert and Felicity Wishes. With her dachshund, Rufus, and her husband, John, she divides her time between Highgate, north London and the north-east. She is the author of a number of short stories, young novels and picture books.

www.helenbaileybooks.com

Life as I know it is going pear-shaped.

Dad's having a mid-life crisis.
Mum's given in to her daytime TV addiction.
My little bro (aka The Little Runt) has just been
caught shoplifting. Even the guinea-pig's gone mental.

And all I can think about is whether green eyeliner
complements or clashes with blue eyes.

I can be **very** shallow.

These are the zits-and-all,
no-holds-barred rants of me,
Electra Brown. Welcome to my crazy world.

Everyone's got major lurve-action except me.

Lucy's had a holiday fling with a bog-brush-headed Frog.

Sorrel's in lust with a lad who reeks of chip fat.

Even the Wundacousin is dating a model, whereas I'm not even getting any befriend-the-ugly-friend attention!

I hate swimming against the tide. I'd rather go with the flow. I should be planning how to hook a hunk, but all I can think is, *What's for lunch?*

I can be **very** shallow.

These are the up-close-and-sometimes-too-personal rants of me, Electra Brown. Welcome to my crazy world.